BEYOND BRIGHTNESS

Sanja Särman

Proverse Hong Kong

Beyond Brightness
by Sanja Särman
Copyright © Proverse Hong Kong December 2016
Alternate pbk edition published in Hong Kong
by Proverse Hong Kong, December 2016
ISBN: 978-988-8228-67-6
Available from: https://www.createspace.com/6616476

First published in pbk in Hong Kong by Proverse Hong Kong,
22 November 2016
Copyright © Proverse Hong Kong November 2016
ISBN: 978-988-8228-35-5

Distribution and other enquiries to:
Proverse Hong Kong, P.O. Box 259, Tung Chung Post Office,
Tung Chung, Lantau Island, NT, Hong Kong SAR, China.
Email: proverse@netvigator.com; Web: www.proversepublishing.com

The right of Sanja Särman to be identified as the author of this work
and of each and every other contributing writer to be identified
as the author of the piece attributed to them in this book
has been asserted by each of them
in accordance with the Copyright, Designs and Patents Act 1988.

Page design, Proverse Hong Kong.
Cover design, Artist Hong Kong Co.
Front cover art and back cover author portait by Sanja Särman.

British Library Cataloguing in Publication Data.
A catalogue record for this book is available
from the British Library.

BEYOND BRIGHTNESS

Sanja Särman

Proverse Hong Kong

Supported by

Hong Kong Arts Development Council

Hong Kong Arts Development Council fully supports freedom of artistic expression. The views and opinions expressed in this project do not represent the stand of the Council.

BEYOND BRIGHTNESS is a succession of tales where characters, many of whom are both sombre and ridiculous, have the sinews of their will cut by the knife of fate, or desire. Särman occasionally seems to be arguing that these phenomena come down to one and the same thing; adducing sentiment as proof. Just as the carbon found in diamonds comes from the living and the dead alike, so dreams, lapses of thought, involuntary visions and sheer boredom are indiscriminately transformed into the gemstone of the special kind of feeling Särman capitalizes on – a feeling which, if it had a name, would be love of fate. "Ave fatum, gratia vidum" is the prayer that resurfaces again and again in this volume, a prayer that asks for no intercession, no screen between oneself and one's destiny. Although the characters are curiously individuated, the centre stage in this book is occupied by Särman's lyrical voice, shot through and through with mystical pain, and the same stubbornly immature longing which characterized Leopardi's "rage to live" in this desert we call the world.

SANJA SÄRMAN is a woman of Sino-Swedish descent. She has two Bachelor Degrees (one in literature and one in philosophy), and one master's degree (philosophy), all three obtained at Uppsala University in Sweden, where she also studied various ancient and modern languages. At the time of writing, she is enrolled as a PhD student at the University of Hong Kong, where she explores moral and literary issues in early modern and late modern philosophy. In addition, she has studied visual arts (drawing and painting) at The Royal Academy of Fine Arts in Brussels and Yunnan Art Institute in China. She mostly paints mythological motifs and portraits. *Beyond Brightness* is her first piece of fiction to be published. She also composes stories and poetry in Swedish and French.

BEYOND BRIGHTNESS
by Sanja Särman

TABLE OF CONTENTS

Tragic Dreams: 7
Preface by Lawrence Gray

Author's Introduction   11

1   The Monist   15
2   Beyond Brightness   25
3   On Whether Sailors Die or Live   33
4   A Trifle Worth Dying For   35
5   As Flies to Wanton Gods   41
6   Eternal Filiation   55
7   Ora et Labora   63
8   The Foundling   67
9   Frieda Roos   81
10   The End of Species   87
11   (One Shade of) Starved Fire   117

Advance Responses   135

Notes   139

PREFACE

Tragic Dreams: *Beyond Brightness*

I am the cheese to Ms Särman's chalk. I write comedies, where the mechanics of life throw up ironies and idiocy. She writes tragedies, where all is mood and misery because our destinies negate all. I operate in the demotic where she operates in the academic mode where one talks of orthography rather than spelling. So when you dip into the world of *Beyond Brightness*, you are a long way away from Anglo-Saxons like P. G. Wodehouse and George Orwell; instead we are among the philosophical Europeans like Proust and Sartre. Be prepared to meet a misty Nordic fairground full of moody existentialists desiring sex and death and an elusive good reason for them.

In her introduction, Sanja Särman mentions Proust, whose notorious opening gambit in *A la recherche du temps perdu* delves exhaustively into the nuances of sleeplessness. One can find the same dreamy half-lit, multi-nuanced world in *Beyond Brightness*. Nobody is in the moment; all are beset by images of pasts, futures, of present fantasies; and like the flats of operatic productions, the scenes slide in and out of the staging. As in all grand operas, we are confronted with wild narrative swings. Here we encounter adolescent girls and older men, Zoroastrian fire and plastic surgery, alien life forms and taxidermy, suicidal children and vomit bloggers, homosexuality and stupid little sluts, the affections of dogs and killer robots, and a constant desire for childhood, or at least the child-welfare officer to halt a father's demand for filial rituals.

Everyone is a dreamer, a contemplative, a meditator, with the concrete world barely existing, except where it is an art form, a piece of music, a fairground ride, the internet! The reality of the characters is simply another's dream. Their own relationships are not a source of comfort or community, but for reflecting upon their own isolation and inevitable death. And nobody likes anyone if they are being kind. Sex and death are the major components of the relationships and the sex is perverse and sadistic. Pain is rarely enough; one must inflict betrayal, one must betray one's father, one must report one's lover to the police, one must get a lover's dog to love one more! And with betrayal there can be death, as one betrayed and imprisoned lover hangs himself and achieves the desired sexual release. Or fails to.

Desire is great in the world of *Beyond Brightness*, but the achievement of what is desired is always a disappointment.

There is a veneer of the east thrown into this collage of imagery and mix of mellifluous words. Sanja refers to the Chinese classic, *The Dream of the Red Chamber*, and Mishima's *The Sea of Fertility*; but whereas in Eastern dramas there is a sense of a fleeting perfection and the inevitable melancholy state at the passing of that moment, in *Beyond Brightness* we are in a place where perfection is never achieved. The end of the world is faced in one of the stories and it will be the biggest humiliation, brought about by endless desires that are ultimately impotent. Singers die. The world is unjust. The sex is unsatisfactory. And the remorse is oceanic. One character has no doubt that God finds her suffering funny. Nothing, as one story says, can be gained by crying out aloud. In the end there is only everlasting separation and an eerie disorientation.

Beyond Brightness is a collection of stories that operate within the zone of the writers that inspired me to write, the Becketts, the Kafkas, the Borges, the Sartres, the Camus, writers unconcerned with traditional story telling but more with the experience of writing and how it enables one to explore moods, feelings, and attitudes towards problems of existence, or, as the Beckett book goes, how it is. These writers never bothered to answer those who asked, What's the story? or Who's your audience? You take or you leave what they write, or should I say, a publicity machine that powerful critics can manufacture presents them to you and then you take or leave them. In comedy, one sees conspiracies and cockups, in tragedy, one is inevitably resigned to one's fate. It will be interesting to see the fate of these stories and how a public respond to them.

Lawrence Gray
Founding President, Hong Kong Writers' Circle
Author of *Odds and Sods*, *Cop Show Heaven*
and *Adam's Franchise*

AUTHOR'S INTRODUCTION

I have often asked myself if tragedy is still possible, or if this short-lived genre was from the very beginning doomed to extinction – if it could last only one century, in Athens. When I have been driven to accept its ephemerality, I have wondered why it must be so. The German philosopher Schelling thought our inability to produce classical tragedy is due to the historical loss of the category of *fate;* in his view, authors of modern tragedy – Shakespeare and Caldéron – have had to reinvent fate. As far as I can see, Schelling understood them to root fate in *character.*

Let us assume that the *fate* of the ancients is impossible today. Must an author who aspires to write tragedy, then, have recourse to character? Let it be noted that I by no means meant to create a full-fledged tragedy in this collection; neither in the individual stories, nor in the overarching whole. Yet, prior to each story there was a wish to probe the land, as it were; to explore the terrain for a kind of contemporary tragedy that does not hinge on *character.* I have wished to replace character with a sometimes ill-fated attachment, an inexplicable urge that, when left unchecked, becomes one's destiny, or karmic sentimentality (緣: yuàn)....

That desire corrodes character, and that this sensuality is tragic, is not my invention; the theme is key to Cao Xueqin's masterpiece *Dream of the Red Chamber.* The outcome of desire's defeat over character is *pain.* And as Mishima, in his tetralogy *The Sea of Fertility*, more or less explicitly shows, this pain is the very *opposite* of character. More subtly, in his *In Search of Lost Time*, Proust –

through the counterpoint of longing, dissolves his characters – such as when, for example, the I realizes the arbitrariness of his preference for Albertine over Andrée. The girls are only pretexts for his longing.

In these short stories, I address the same issue as these authors have addressed, but in a much more humble form, and in a much lower key. In so doing I wish to show how some of our most everyday pain may be elevated to the height of tragedy. Each story is to be taken as the emotional setting for a possible tragedy.

THE MONIST

I

I had been in Hong Kong for a while. I had taken the escalator uphill as *kulis* were pulling their barrows and wagons below me; they were not allowed to transport their merchandise (always something like an oily metallic cylinder) where I travelled. They did not work in factories: incinerators did not recruit them, they were not allowed to sully manufactured goods, especially not electronic devices. They carried, towed, and pulled, as they had always done.

On the same steep slope where so many overpriced Western restaurants were strewn, where hipsters desperately clung to their laptops and smartphones, the *kulis* still laboured, often bare-chested: the sinewy muscles of these immortal beasts of draught glistened with sweat as they pierced the smoke cloud that emanated from the cigars. I say immortal – because I had not before contemplated the extent to which this civilization was erected on their bodies; how deep their ancestors laid buried in their monuments. The great wall was really made of flesh: the Chinese anthem had not falsely advertised it. Perhaps this was the case everywhere – but in Europe, where I came from, labour was usually not so overtly bloody, not so blatantly bitter. Their strength was truly bitter: in comparison, my weakness was sweet, as I sailed above them on the travellator, past the pastel skyscrapers, on my way to the Cathedral.

I would that it were otherwise: that another possibility had realized itself on this hilly country; that we had not – to such an extent at least – thrived on their sweat. But unlike many others I was not convinced I knew what I meant when I made this wish. For I had never experienced a "possibility", and the exact reduplication of the sky in the sea, and the delirious sadness of its blue, made me more convinced than ever that I would always be steeped in reality. There was no escaping the shady monochrome of the sky, marbled in purple and white... Heaven had descended on earth, or at least, its hue had. If I had not been necessitated to come, I surely would not have: but I had, and hence I was necessarily here – just like the light of the invisible sun in the sky was necessarily everywhere.

I had been in Hong Kong for a while. I had seen the mist invade at night, and in the soft haze the electric lights looked back at me: greenish glow-worms on violet cargo vessels.... Then the sunset had dragged its long fingers through the vault, now marked with parallel tints of orange and cobalt.

I was an assistant professor at an economy school and for some reason quite popular among the students; I was always mocked by my female colleague, Cookie Lee, for the number of girls who cried in my office. She had never resorted to such means of self-paternalization, she said, even though she had chosen the name Cookie for herself. So I married her.

In marrying her I acquired all of her interests, because I had almost none of my own. She played the *guzhen*, and took me along to concerts; she photographed flowers, and tried to awaken my respect for these brittle beings; she sang; danced; cooked, and as a consequence I had to observe, applaud and eat. I had soon no leisure time to spare for the melancholy into which I always lapsed when left on my own.

I had not expected this side-effect.

That day I had been to the zoo with the by now pregnant Cookie, and seen the blue crane drag its tail – black as if dripping with ink – in the dust, and the flamingos wallowing in perfectly circular, artificial ponds, filled with a pigment that looked like red ochre. Although the land turtle had not sought refuge in the small pagoda, the monkeys had covered their faces with shame. On humid nights, I had seen the banyan trees with their sky-reaching root systems, so desperately entwined as to be an almost ridiculously perfect symbol of human affection.... And now I admired them with Cookie.

Cookie was also interested in traditional Chinese opera: in Beijing opera as well as in its less elegant Cantonese counterpart. And now she had taken me to a concert. I protested half-heartedly: was it necessary to attend the zoo and the opera on one wretched day? Why not stay at home, take a bath and watch some TV instead...?

"*You are the monist,*" she said. "*You* know they're really the same."

So I accompanied her.

"I would follow Cookie anywhere" – in vain I tried to excuse my weakness of will by *affection*.

***

A word like "opera" surely has grandiose connotations. This was no opera, I immediately noted. The orchestra consisted of only a few players. The singers did not even wear proper costumes, only some tasteless outfits that they had thought appropriate. "It's really like the zoo," I thought, when a young man – but certainly no boy, entered the "stage", dressed in a jacket, with prints in the iridescent blue and green of a peacock's plumage. My wife hurriedly explained that he was to perform the *dan*-role: the role of the concubine, the palace maid, or whoever was, like them, sufficiently heartbroken and brave.

He put his head on one side and – *chirped,* but a chirp that had been magnified a hundredfold: his throat was like the bowstring on which an arrow dripping with poison trembled for a moment, before it was discharged and pierced my heart.

Listening to his nasal falsetto, I did my best to rid myself of the overtones of irony I could not help detecting in it. As of late, I had had the impression that people thought themselves dignified only to the extent that they remained indifferent in face of the *affected,* and I did not want to fall prey to this easy superiority. In some glorious past, the exaggeration of a gesture had not contradicted the dignity of its executor: we were now as immune to irony as they had once been. I did not cover my ears.

Listening to this song, I suddenly remembered what it had been like to be seventeen years old. Along endless waters I staggered until finally I would fall asleep against a pebbledash wall. I followed the rails till I fainted. I wished I would drop dead on every field of oats I saw. Everything that was desolate seemed to be a battlefield where the powers of my soul carried out their incomprehensible showdowns.

I roamed for days in the suburbs, eating left-over pizza slices from paper trays and chocolate I found in the gutter, I roamed until at last I met a man who seemed to be armed – not necessarily with knives and guns. Poles, wires and saws; oars, hooks or even harpoons, anything, and I ... I was overjoyed with fear. Yet I took pains not to fantasize – I never fantasized. To this day I have never imagined anything even remotely sensual; I have never undressed a woman in my imagination, and, not even when I marvelled at the bleeding knuckles of a fighter did I ever think about the spot they stained. I refuse to speculate. Even though I ... rejoiced at the sight of them, I refused to speculate on where his fists were destined to hit: and never did I imagine being their destiny. My anticipation of violence was different. I sustained it stubbornly, yet I never specified it. I still do not know what I hoped for: I still do not know whether I hoped or feared.

Although I did not believe in God back then, I never doubted that *desire* had been apportioned to each of us according to our deserts. And if mine had been vague from the onslaught – if mine would never assume a form of any kind – if I would never dream of a body or a sequence of sensations – I would still stand by it, to the end. I could but remain true to my yearning; mine was the feverish loyalty of the pervert. I had no choice but to wander and anticipate a lethal pain in my neck – a pain that never came. And as I grew older, I forgot what that was like.

I forgot what it was like to wander aimlessly, heavy with overindulged expectation, taking pains to keep this expectation open and imprecise. Even though I dared not think about being robbed, raped, stabbed and tucked away, I hoped – not for *it*, but for whatever *greater misery* of which all these assaults were but tokens; I hoped for that greater rapture which has no name, *for which I refused to have a name,* because a name would tarnish the purity of my anticipation. If I had a name for it, I would know when my hopes were dashed; I would know where to go to avoid or welcome *it*; I would call *it* by its proper name, and that was surely sacrilege.

I was hoping for it throughout my teens. Never again had I grazed the vicinities of this sad, sad exhilaration. No high wire act, no high risk prostitute had brought it back, and I had forgotten that once *that* had been all I lived for. I had married a beautiful woman who only occasionally embedded her polished nails in the small of my back; she would never administer the total and formless defeat that spellbound me for years. I had forgotten how important it was, to suffer *in an unknown way at the hands of an unknown creature*!

And yet – here it was, the danger: it was wholly expressed by the vibration of his vocal chords; the risk of staying alive comprised in that incredibly unnerving falsetto.

At seventeen years, what I feared most of all was perhaps the impossibility of rape. I feared that the ravishment of the Sabines was nothing but legend: perhaps no-one had ever been *wronged.* Perhaps there was an interiority that would always defeat all violent attempts at unification; a kernel lodged so deep that even the *soul* was only its brittle shell. A kernel so holy that I could never rid myself of it. I wanted to expose myself *wholly* to the vagaries of chance: I wanted to disprove this possibility.

His voice, too, prayed that at least the force that oppressed it was true, and not merely a dream. It expressed the same *disgusted integrity* that had caused me to wander back then. The palace maid sang as if she was aware that in the end, she was not imprisoned in the palace, but the palace imprisoned in her. She wanted to denounce this captivity, but she could not: her soul was too large, *all* was necessarily confined in it. Only the generous, only the big-hearted know this melancholy; and no-one is more generous than the incarcerated. They waste all their richness on *any old walls*.

When the performance was over, my wife almost instantly went to congratulate the singer; they discussed technical details of which I only understood a small fraction. But from the close distance, I saw how his powder was coming off in flakes. And it was then I realized that countless men in history, my predecessors, had fallen for this feminine artifice – that femininity was but an artifice, his as well as my own, and, even worse: I realized that we would never cease to fall – *fall* for this imaginary weakness.

II

When the cleaning lady cleaned, I dared not exit. I sat by my desk and heard all the mundane sounds: the vacuum cleaner; the mopping; the evacuation of the trash…. I saw a white boat plough its barren furrow of foam in the sea. I saw the powdery pink skyscrapers turn purple in the rain. I childishly refused to leave my sanctuary at my desk. She knew it had to be dirty in here. I claimed that I could not think otherwise; I pretended my thought was the crystallization of the dirt around me.

I heard her speak Filipino on the phone. She spoke loudly and laughed a lot. I was sure she spoke of me.

I was imprisoned there, until Cookie came. Then I begged her: could we not invite the singer for dinner. She conceded; but I could see that she knew already. She conceded only because she knew that he was above me, and that I could never come close.

Never before had I been so self-conscious as I was when at last we were together again, in the dim red light in the restaurant of his choice – that my face was so square, that I had shaved myself poorly, unevenly: that there were dark spots on my cheeks, that the cut-glass chandelier was reflected in my rectangular glasses, that it gleamed there like a flickering desire…. Of course I had to be dressed in a checkered shirt, the colours were hopeless: lemon yellow, blue and black.

I had not had lunch that day; I ate too much, too fast; I pierced the turnip cake with my chopstick and bit a piece off; some of it fell back on the plate. Cookie looked aghast.

He was picky, of course. He liberated the goji seeds from the slimy interior of the osmanthus-cake and swallowed them slowly. He looked bored and sick. He took the porcelain cup with index finger, middle finger and thumb: I stared at it as if I had expected something else. His head was too big; his shoulders folded and his breast concave. He deigned not look at me as I gulped. He looked away, through the window, at the curtain of rain. His skin was the colour of rain.

Cookie conversed with the female singers in his troop. There were two of them. He did not even pretend to listen to them. As in prayer, he joined the palms of his hands together and rested his chin on the tips of the middle fingers; placing the elbows on the table. But time and again he would laugh; I could see how the women were fuelled by his mirth: how it spurred them on; they tried to out-rival each other in wittiness. Soon enough, the conversation became absurd. I had not seen Cookie so giddy for years, and she had not even tasted the wine. *I* could never whip up an atmosphere with a smile; my laughter was not worth their nonsensical jokes. On my lot fell – alas – dignified comments, wisdom, self-ironical authority.... I did not know how to behave in this chaos of sopranic giggles accompanied by the clink of their jewelry: I felt like a hunter defeated by the explosion of feathers provoked by his well-aimed shot.... I had less and less to say.

I had nothing to say.

I was so speechless I could cry. I excused myself – nobody paid me any attention – and went to the W.C. for the purpose of crying a little; but as I stood before the hanging mirror, gripping the sink, preparing to face my reflection – he entered. Again, he did not look in my direction, and as he passed by, he was careful not to brush against me; he slanted his waist inwards, as gracious as an odalisque avoiding the grasp of her drunken master – and I could not help inhaling. The combination of sugar, *eau de cologne*, grease, preserved flowers and sperm was dazzling. When young men – not boys – were close enough to me, I always instinctively inhaled their odour: I was confident I could live off the carbon dioxide they emitted. Their breath would be both impoverished and perfumed.

I had hoped he would ask me something concerning my area of expertise – the expansion of superpowers in the area spanned by the so-called Cow Tongue in the South China Sea, the threats of war, something about naval bases forming interlinked strings of beads.... I had delivered so many papers at so many conferences: I was used to being the cosmopolitan scholar, committed to no side, free and floating, sometimes even sharp. Now I shuddered at the prospect of him bringing up my lowly research. His lowered eyes conveyed that not only was I a stranger to his country: up till now I had not even known what a country was, or what could hold it together.... Only the voices of dead singers can…. The voices of dead singers! One silence more legendary than the other! Death! Aspiring to become a silence in their midst: aspiring to become the voice for which one mistakes the rustling of the leaves, once the body is gone. "Is that him? No: it was only the soaring of an eagle sinking in the sea…." Singers die. The world is unjust.

I really had nothing to say.

When I paid he looked as disgusted as if he could spit at me, and then, he gave me his card.

III

His house was even smaller than my first apartment in Hong Kong had been.

We drank in silence for almost one hour. I wanted to tell him that his voice had reminded me of a silken muzzle stained with a drop of blood. Instead, I trapped his wrist between his shoulders, and pulled it upwards until he knelt. He knelt. He really knelt. But then he told me to let go.

I left overcome with shame. For I had brought to his knees the man who had the voice of my imaginary killer. I had humiliated him, and myself – as all of us must do who can neither bleed nor be grateful for the blood of others: the blood that has cemented this pavement; the air that bleeds from the strokes of that voice.

I knew not what I wished for when I would that it were otherwise: that songs were not always so sad, and the poor not always so naked. But I wished! And my wish was as imprecise as my desire, this desire that could be fulfilled as little as a disembodied voice could be brought to its knees. At last I knew why I, long ago, had longed to drown in every golden field I passed by – to be crushed by the shadows cast by the clouds – and since then, I could never again forget what it had been like to be seventeen years old.

BEYOND BRIGHTNESS

❛❛I sit on the admissions board of the university of N. If you apply I will ensure that your application is given ... special consideration," said he, and looked deep into Alexandra's eyes. He's American – I can't be more specific – because only American scholars tour the globe on the hunt for gifted, convertible lesbians. She's Swedish, but of Asian descent and with "exotically" slanted eyes from which gush, in flashes, a mortifying clarity. Her eyes expel the clarity in which she basks, as if her body can't sustain its own excess of inner light. Without perspicacity *he* couldn't go on living: imagine wasting away in self-conceited confusion; imagine never acknowledging a holy desire. There's something sacramental about an earnest attempt at seduction, at least when displayed by someone so rotten, she notes.

He said, "If you write an abstract by December 31, I'll see to it that you can join our laboratory at the university of N. You'll be challenged then, *surely for the first time*, so you'll have to make an effort." Did he just make a pun on her, at last, losing her conative virginity?

"But I don't want to make an effort."

"So that's your problem, then," he observed and passed her the wine-list. To please him, she ordered the most expensive bottle. Like all men that spoil too eagerly their prey, he was convinced that they wouldn't love him for his own sake. Sadly, he was right. When he was in the men's room, she jotted down a line in her notebook: *Dining with a heartbreakingly indulgent pervert*, and since her period was a-coming, she would have cried at that, had she been alone.

He didn't ask what she wanted instead of efforts: why would he? It is pointless to ask how people would react if they knew that all you want is to enact a fantasy, and not even an indecent one.

"I've prepared a gift for you," he said. "But I left it in the hotel."

"Bring it next week," she proposed. With transatlantic transparency, he declared that impossible: what if the other students spotted the proof of his misplaced tenderness? Or even worse, a scholar, whose circuit between impression and judgment had been perfected by scientific training. This could threaten their deliberations, perhaps even render him incapable of elevating her to his side.

His hotel room was an ideal scene for the extinction of a young personality. The wall-paper was of a powdery pastel blue, a colour that is in itself an infantile erotic nightmare. The noise from the railway station reverberated faintly. The decorated destitution of this room rendered in spatial form his raising pulse, his hollow ecstasy.

His teeth glistened with saliva as he spoke on the advantages that the perusal of the volume had lent him and *other* great men like himself. Then he placed the gift in her hands. He gave away too early that it was a book; he was too eager to exhibit the thoughtfulness behind his choice. Certainly this plan had been contrived in haste; maybe it was the only decent book left on the shelf.

She tore asunder the cellophane wrapping and said, "I've already read Plutarch."

"You're not being polite. It's a gift, you know," he corrected her.

"Well, thank you: I don't doubt that I'll find it rewarding," she mumbled, procuring a vibrating cellphone from her chest pocket. She always kept it there back then; it was as if it had knocked on her heart.

She glanced at the text message and a cohort of hitherto extinct feelings revived. It was from her mother and read, "I miss you." This feigned maternity made her long for the kind of dependency upon another being from which you can never recover: for a moment, she wished for a primordial surrender to engulf all later inventions of love and contempt. This instant was enough to make her sway a little, and he had her seated on the hard starched hotel bed. She excused herself, saying that her mother had temporarily re-emerged; a mother whom she'd declared dead some years ago. She even notified him that there had been some abuse, because in principle she thought one should cling to aging parents. When all is said and done, there is no other measure of the strength of a character than the proximity it assumes to its own decaying source.

"That's fine," he said. "All interesting women I've met have had horrible mothers. A woman is more or less a wound caused by another woman. That's called birth, I believe."

"So what are men, then?"

"Unborn...." Then he added, cajolingly, "Don't despise me."

"I don't despise," she lied.

They spoke awkwardly of affiliation. He wanted to impart an inarticulate lesson. His father had not really been a father: only the soreness of an ancient wound inflicted on humanity by nature. Curse this necessity for all you want, but don't expect it to be anything but sore. Slowly, as if step by step, he had learnt to rejoice in this.

"You're right, I'm very grateful, I am. Luckier than most...." And instinctively, she traced with her fingertips the many fat scars in the curve of her back. Protruding furrows where happiness had been sown. But when the chill fingers of the professor tried to entangle with hers, as she redrew the contours of a joy written in her skin, she slapped them. Instantly he withdrew.

"You don't like compliments, do you?" he softly begged.

"I don't," she confirmed.

"Would you prefer it if I called you dumb?" he asked, and spurred on by her flinching, pursued, "Pretty but dumb, a stupid little slut."

In principle, she would indeed have preferred that – but the irony of him painstakingly wooing her, even to the point where he would insult her easiness, could hardly be endured.

Was it not too early on in their so-called romance for him to insult her like this? They hadn't even kissed. She pitied him so much that she let him play a little with her hair. He himself was balding in a not too flattering way. There was no submission in her pity; nor was there any ruthlessness when suddenly his pants flung open.

He had wound a lock of her hair around two of his fingers; she disentangled it and prepared to leave. A flapping damp sound was already emerging, so she turned her back on him and approached the door. Then she decided that she might as well await his release. It was too late to inform him that this hands-on exorcism wouldn't chase away the demon. It was too late to infringe on what had lately become a sort of *right* of his, an inalienable right of self-gratification. She advanced to the window from which she spotted the perspective of flight erected by the rusty rails. Trails of blood left behind by something destined to die *elsewhere*.

But he wasn't released of his light burden. Not even close. The living dew remained within him, like repressed tears. He buttoned his pants, relentlessly apologizing. In his eyes she spotted a buoyant panic. Their whites were lilac in the dim light.

His gallantry, interspersed with bribes, had gone on for as long as she took his lectures. His oratorical performance was of a stunningly unequal quality. His unpredictability was not due to that good, old eccentricity you seek in your teachers when you first enroll at university, and that you conjure up when it's clearly absent.... His register was wider than most, but his tones hardly purer. He *would* abuse the wayward youth that took his courses, if he could; but the remorse he suffered afterwards was worse than their trauma: it was oceanic. Intelligence aside, he could laugh harder, cut deeper into living flesh and blush hotter than any man she'd met before. And he thought that would be enough to win her over.

Now it had come down to this. To this dry, barren and laughable catastrophe.

Later on, a young woman, proudly declaring herself a victim of his adulterous scheme, outed him in what she called a petition. Evidently, the old man had promised her to leave his spouse and join her, which made Alexandra titter. He couldn't be imagined without his wife, his pool, his eternally adolescent children and his two overfed dogs. A no doubt accurate vision of him now, imprisoned behind suburban, trellised roses, had already quenched Alexandra's need for vengeance. There was no tenure in his lasciviousness; he didn't have the spine of an old poet who pursues to the end of the world his lover's smooth buttocks. Even his exploitation was essentially curbed: how could this have taken anyone by surprise?

In Alexandra's branch of science, you were expected to praise the victim for her bravery. But Alexandra couldn't stomach the style of the denunciation: it was so numb and yet so spiteful, desperately extolling hymeneal exclusivity after having failed to rob his wife of it. Relations, as the petition envisaged them, were such poor constellations, cemented by jealousy alone, that Alexandra felt she could grow sterile only by reading about it.

Most of the girls brought to sign it were tiny, sinewy, still oozing of delayed puberty; his tastes were distastefully exposed. He had offered them *everything* and thankfully accepted whatever they could give in return. He doted on creatures for whom a fellowship, or even a publication, was critical; they either had to succeed now, or abandon *thinking* altogether and resign from their noble intellectual pursuits, be transformed into administrative personnel in labyrinthine corporations and monthly send their parents a deserving portion of their offspring's income. And he thought it pleased these young women immensely when he complimented them on their intelligence. He loved calling vain children bright, and maybe vanity is a kind of brightness. At the very least, it is elementary to our survival.

Her girlfriend knew what Alexandra had been through and insisted that she too should sign it. But Alexandra could not think of anything more saddening than this band of incompetent youths, encircling their old benefactor, taking turns at clawing his humbly bare head, at blinding the meek eyes that already pierced so little.

"He's unable even to masturbate, let alone rape," she protested with compassion. "He came at me in earnest, as if he were to denounce himself...."

He hadn't forced her into anything. He would never do anything but manipulate her: not because rapture collided with his moral standards but because it opposed his vanity. This vanity that was now to be irrevocably crushed in the wake of endless litigations. Perhaps the accusations would, in the end, turn him into the monster they invoked.

"But in his position, to wield that kind of power over young minds that easily bend. Do you condone that? Do you find it excusable? If you study his case more clearly, you will see that he should be persecuted for what he has done."

"Since when is it illegal to be rejected?"

Alexandra thought of the mercies Persian princes had bestowed on their admiring slaves. She thought of the traitorous demon who prior to his execution by sword had been allowed to kiss the prince's shoulder, as white and smooth as pomegranate blossoms...

What lousy favours authority still keeps: how sullied are the gifts it can still afford to waste! The only thing disgraceful about this affair, Alexandra thought, is the poverty of his lavishness; he offered them all he had, but that came close to *nothing*.

So what if a young brittle thing, on one unique occasion, had been lured into his lair, as she tried in vain to catch a piece of gold that he'd attached to a string? To each her snare!

Try as she might, though, Alexandra couldn't believe that all stupidity in the world could add up to the success of that trap: the would-be victims must have had other motives, as culpable as his. Some might have been enthralled by the pale aura surrounding him; some might have mistaken his despair for genius. This inextricable knot of exploitation they were now to sever for their own lethal gratification. *Lethal*, because, certainly, we live only insofar as we acquit.

"No, listen!" she prays her girlfriend. He had not raped her. In vain she tries to impart the holy involuntary clarity by which she *sees* his innocence. She feels as if her eyes were microscopic lenses in some divine experiment. That the organs of sight should also be a means of seduction! That we should be seen and estimated according to our *eyes*!

That, surely, is justice.

"But, love, he harassed you," her girlfriend, beautiful and vigilant, corrects her. The transparency of her knightliness, of all knightliness, for once appears a bit sickening.

"You don't understand," Alexandra answers. "I wasn't harassed. I'll never be."

If anything, she had been raped by the clarity in her own eyes.

ON WHETHER SAILORS LIVE OR DIE

Maria pouted, but did not accuse. "I expected it," she said. I feared that the mortification I felt at this would soon transform into a rage. Now, I was furiously braiding my fringe, tearing at a wisp of hair. "I knew you'd be back," Maria added, and I felt that I wanted to wreck her body, a body I had owned from stem to stem, that I had bent in all joints, one after another, but that was now so rigid and self-righteous. I had wanted to apologize, but since Maria had responded to my return like this – with the excruciating matter-of-factness of a saint – I couldn't.

"You'll always be back, Liz," she said conceitedly. Her pupils were widened by love, as dark as the sea at night; and I suddenly realized why Anacharsis, to the question whether the dead or the living were most in number, had responded, "To which category, then, do you count those on the sea?" The beholder of Maria's eyes led an equally undecided existence.

She was the only lover I ever had, whom I could leave without stating a purpose, and be back together with, forever. She was also the only one who would never find it touching, not in the slightest, who would never come up with metaphors to numb the betrayal, using words like "will-o'-the-wisp" or "fading lights". She would wait in doglike humility, without excusing her mistress. Did I know enough about dogs to be qualified to use this hackneyed expression?

As a matter of fact, I had brought my own dog this time, a greyhound mix…. A magnificent hound to be honest; it was probably half borzoi, half greyhound, although you never know for sure with dogs from the pound. Although it was always calm, borderline mellow, Maria was slowly working it into a rage. She teased it with toys: she did not let go of them; they kept trailing back and forth on the carpet; they squiggled and squeaked, making the awful noise of trivial creatures dying. She would not let go, although the dog clawed at her hand, and bit it. The dog was playful but troubled; it wanted to rest, but she kept coming at it with all kitsch pet stimuli she could find in the wardrobe – for her parents' spoilt schnauzer had recently died of cancer, and for some reason they had stowed away all its belongings. My dog looked at me; it was ashamed that the make-believe death throes of the toys made it lunge at them; instinct obliged it to do so.

And watching it bite Maria's hands, I felt as awkward as the description of a female character's insecurity over some insignificant bodily flaw in a novella by a male author. Of course neither Maria nor I had ever wished for the body parts of *another*; we were human beings after all, and not blueprints for androids.

"Stop," I begged as the dog's fangs playfully pierced the skin of my lover. It drew blood.

But Maria smiled: her front teeth were full and protruding, and perfectly white. Maria knew that this way she would trick the dog into loving her. Maria's patience which had lain in ambush for so long finally overpowered me. My dogs would always love Maria more, as would all the world: as I always will. We will always love the nestled bones of lovers in prehistoric graves; we will always find the swan the superior singer, even when it croaks – because we imagine that it loves to die. She laughed as I scolded the dog; and even louder as I placed ice cubes on the drop that lay crushed on the carpet – for as all housewives know, once the blood is heated, the stain remains.

A TRIFLE WORTH DYING FOR

We meet in a coffeehouse – one of those living-room-like ones, with red velvet armchairs and lamps on tables fashioned like piles of old books.

Cupboards of plastic looking like wood. Unbelievable. For our last exchange of intimacy to take place in this strained coziness....

She wore a black pleated skirt, a sweater so high that you could spot her belly button when she stood up, and lace-up sandals.

"I'm sorry I'm late. I'm in love."

"With whom?"

She tucked away her tissue and described to me the character of the high-strung old libertine whom she had settled for. Of course it was her boss, an elegant swine that I had met once.

"He knows I have a soul, but only tells me to shut up and obey. He is not one of those men whose insecurities you slowly unwrap, as if they were Christmas gifts, one of those whom you redeem with your patience, who at last break down in your arms. Oh, no! No. His gaze told me that if I ever came close to his *source*, he would cut me to pieces and bury me somewhere, never to be found. He is cocooned in crystalline strength, untouchable, and so eager to touch.

He is all hell-bound superficiality and strong fingers, spitting at high-chested beauties since the dawn of time, a factory of humiliation mass-producing graces for bitches like me.

You know, they tell me his wife is younger than me, and submissive as a concubine. So what could I offer him that he does not already enjoy? Only fire, insanity and my special breed of quirky insatiability in bed. Will that be enough?"

What could I say? "Dea," I said. "Don't make a fool of yourself. When has that ever been enough?" She laughed, for too long. She prided herself on being insufficient in love. Years ago, I would have asked myself why this once sharp-witted young lady would struggle so much to pose as a pain-crazed sex-toy, but I no longer thought such musings worth the effort. Some people crave for nothing else in life than to declare before the incredulous masses that they come from outer space. "I am," they insist when confronted, "I *am* an alien. I'm nothing like you at all." And the more we doubt them, the more they will try to prove us wrong.

She went on, "I care nothing about furniture, family, career, love, holidays, money, food, clothes, cosmetics, belongings, books, culture, art, nature, religion, goodness or truth. I don't care about my friends, especially not about you. I don't care about my feelings, happiness, wisdom or beauty. I don't. I really don't." She was waiting for me to get irritated and finally ask, "So what do you care about then?" Then, at last, she could give her preposterous answer. It would be one word, of course. It would be one word, not an indecent one, and she would utter it in a whisper with down-cast eyes. That way she thought she could command our pity. In the past, she used to do that to me too, and sooner or later, overwhelmed, I would have to sleep with her. But now I didn't ask, and it amused me to observe her as she pursued her train of thought unaided by my interest.

"I've always pitied ... " she said, "... I've always pitied perverts who desire something irreversible, who fancy being hanged or beheaded. Because when at last they enact it, they are more exposed to the vagaries of chance than the others, who just wish to perpetuate the species. Because at last, when they enact it – and trust me, they will! – they are doomed to such a *capital* disappointment. In a glimpse they might see how profoundly unsatisfactory dying is.... The moment that sustained them all their lives will hurt them with its ugliness as they wriggle helplessly, hanging high. And there will be no second go. Just one life-long fever and one final disappointment."

"What do you know?" I asked her. "What do you know about dying? It might be as glorious as the martyrs pretend."

Disputing the authority with which she spontaneously spoke on matters of death annoyed her. Always, when on the verge of suicide, she would turn about and slap the person who encouraged her across the mouth. She sipped on her latte, enraged.

"*What do I know,*" she repeated. "What do I know about death. I fucking am death."

Death? Ms Death? An alien sex-slave in dandruff-powdered black? A trembling insomniac whose IQ had decreased by two standard deviations in one year, and was dropping steadily still? A bimbo with bloodshot eyes, a knack for unconscious rambling and an unmatched taste for ribaldry, all of which, combined, made her lovers mistake her for a poet – I could never forget when she betrayed me with a monster so huge that he, as she said, *reached her heart from within....* A girl – at last – a girl whose wrists were twiggier than those of any other girl I've ever met, a girl who daily replaced at least one meal with ice-cream and chocolate? You don't look like death to me: quite the contrary.... But I didn't say a word.

"Hilary," she suddenly confessed, "I can't live on my own."

I swallowed. She had lived with me for a while, but two years ago, we had split up. I had done all the cooking, the cleaning, the laundry, the groceries, the tidying-up; I had even cut her fringe for her, although she had been unhappy with the result. And in return, I had received the worst sex of my life. She had not even watered my plants, and my most beautiful orchids had died.

"Look," I said, evasively.... There was nothing there to look at. A few teenagers passed by, an Indian businessman, a limping German shepherd on a leash. The wind was tearing at some black plastic above a Western Union sign. It fluttered subtly in the gushes of air from the cars that drove by. The wind was cold. Long gone were the days when you could expect warmth in May. Yet, the air-conditioning was on, constantly buzzing, like a homophonous choir of coldness. A poor boy with a trolley passed by. An old man with a towel about his neck. Look, Dea, at all these people. They work. They live. They love. Why can't you be a little like them? All suggestions accepted.

"Can I come home?" she finally asked. Although I didn't look at her, I knew she was tearing at the skin around her fingernails. Years ago, I would have told her to stop fretting about things. I would have held her down. Be calm, I would have said. Not anymore.

"Then I know what I must do," she said. I nodded. She must, before it was too late, transform all her fantasies to intercessions. It could be done, for sure. She had never doubted that God found her suffering funny. In this sense, at least, she had never lost faith, and therefore she had retained, despite her inborn blasphemy, the capacity to pray.

"Good luck," I said. She got up in a rush, struggled to disentangle her handbag from the chair, and walked away. Her left foot tipped inwards as she walked. She was upright as a soldier but still crept on tip-toe, as if not to disturb someone.

Her awkward gait was still endearing: in a few years time it would only be disgustingly immature, I thought.

And for one strange moment, I wished for her what she wished for herself: abduction, transfiguration, perfect success in the alchemy of seduction; for her to metamorphose into a constellation transfixed above my head, for her name to be written in fire across the heavens – and for herself to be gone. Gone before the decay of a life wasted on imperceptible sacrifices would ruin her face. Gone in May, before the monsoons would soak her. For her to be gone.

***

The last time I heard about her, she was said to have returned to her home planet. And sometimes, in my dreams, she arrives at my windowsill in a small vessel, she speaks of holidays spent on the rings of Saturn, she sheds her human costume, and stands before me: resplendent, coy and silly, truly an angel of death.

AS FLIES TO WANTON GODS

The amateur boxer spoke ardently of Muhammed Ali. Electra knew little; only that he, too, had been "charismatic" in the sense that you would like to bend your knee before him, with your hands tied.... Oh, Muhammed Ali: the crazy stuff lesser men pay prostitutes to hurl at them in bed, he had the whole world singing. *He was the greatest.* Like most great artists, he fought against oblivion – not that of the world, which he knew was marked forever – but against his own; slowly he tumbled into it, and was swallowed by the darkness in which his own sermons could no longer reach him. In his burning, and sometimes blind, antagonism, Ali had been like an angel, flaying us prematurely for our crime – exacting in life part of our eternal punishment, and that was why white intellectuals like Norman Mailer loved him so much. They found his presence purging.

Electra thought she had now at last met a man who like him seemed an enfleshed cell in purgatory, a foretaste of divine suffering, ready to lock you in a stifling embrace. Back then, she had the habit of being picked up, making out and then suddenly refusing to go further.

She was convinced she had been born to amplify beyond all measure the ego of *one man.* Such a pity she could never remember who he was. That was, perhaps, why she, after all the initial furrowing, suddenly recoiled, frozen in sullen amnesia, as they stood before her, arms akimbo, penis sagging, waiting for the condom to drop off. She almost enjoyed to hear them exclaim, *"So what now?"* – because, sooner or later, we always come to enjoy the expected outcome. And that is why one should never expect anything but endless glory.

Since she was accustomed to it, she found their expressions – all short-circuited libido, all tremendous self-accusation, all tenderness, amusing. Most of them would acquiesce in this inexplicable flash of chastity: after all, she didn't owe them anything, she was just another mechanism forfeiting the pleasures of the night, just another element in that clockwork of bad luck that never stopped ticking in their minds. Upon *"So what now?"*, they usually made her bed, and in their sleep she would observe them, as still as raw marble blocks unaware of the shapes they habour. Sometimes they would turn their backs at her, and she and her would-be lover would sleep with their spines almost intertwining.

But if Sanjo could not, this time, screw her, he wouldn't simply go to bed: what could there be for them between those rustling sheets? To wake up again and again, soaked with the dew of nightmares, Electra out of reach by your side, what a torturous, never-ending night. Instead, he bade her watch the storm from his open window; she ducked and clutched at the windowsill for fear; at last she got to press her front against a prophetic knee, by accident and all.

In the formless mass of purple clouds, she saw the lightning strike: at once, the muscles and veins of the enlightened clouds were shrouded in almost hysterical clarity; only the lower segment of the sickly moon could be spotted, its reclining crescent a condescending smile. They still could not hear the thunder. The atmosphere was so oppressive that any whiff of sulphur would amount to a liberation. She said she was afraid; he said there was nothing to fear. Indeed, the storm did not unclench over them; that night, there was no release. Only in the afternoon, the following day, did the wind finally begin to move the heavy clouds, with their cobalt-lining, in the direction of his mezzanine.

Spurred on by the storm, they tried again. But for some reason she panicked.

"*Honey!*" he exclaimed (he was Tibetan, from the Qinghai province; since Electra spoke Mandarin so poorly, they had recourse to English, and his stock of pet names was limited to this one word). "What have you been through, to become like this? Were you hurt?"

"Never," she said, sadly, "I'm invulnerable."

Since they could not make it, Sanjo recited some poetry from the *Songs of Chu*, seemingly written in honour of this very sort of anticlimax. Electra felt like hitting him. "Why must it all be so very sad?" she asked.

He smiled, and said, "To the ancients, sorrow and beauty were one and the same thing. *You* ought to know this. That, more than anything, proves their superiority: they could endure so much pain that they confused the stirrings of sorrow with the sting of beauty. They were like that, all of them; we're nowhere close."

So, little by little, he gave away that he was a poet, too. She prayed in silence he would not recite any of his verses to her. Especially if he'd composed them in English, awaiting an "international audience" like herself, for her mother was from Glasgow and her father from Hong Kong, she would find it too embarrassing. To avert this, she asked him about his past.

Sanjo had been a monk once. He revealed it just as you would expect, without a trace of nostalgia.

Like Samuel came to Eli, after he'd been awakened by the voice of God calling his name – a voice that I've always imagined to be something like that of a smoking preacher: hoarse, regretful and infinitely tender, Sanjo had gone to see his guru in the middle of the night – an infraction, of course. Unlike in Samuel's case, however, there had been no voice; staring at a *thangka* and then falling asleep, Sanjo had *seen* the flaming wheel of existence, and sensed the mysterious causality behind our suffering. And he knew he would never again be in position to execute the tonglen breathing technique, wherein suffering is inhaled, and what little joy you've *earned* (because all happiness is truly merited, it is, and only the weak are immune to this truth) exhaled unto them, who have never earned it, and never will. He didn't wish to exchange his serenity for their gratuitous pain; he did not want to become a Bodhisattva anymore.

No, he wasn't exactly indifferent to other sentient beings; he didn't blame them for being crushed again and again by the ever-spinning wheel of reincarnation, by the logical punishment of life, *but still* ... he didn't want to waste his own liberation *on them*. He abandoned them without declaring their salvation a lost cause. He didn't have the pretext of someone like Luther – who, to all appearances, didn't believe in the efficacy of intercession or indulgence. Sanjo's problem was that he believed in these (or, rather, in their Buddhist counterparts) much *too vividly*, even though, on a cognitive level, he didn't believe that much at all.

Often, he dissected himself as a believer; he saw himself – Sanjo, the believer – through the lens of the intrinsically irreligious science of psychology; it was the 21st century after all, and he was fostered in a tradition erected on the twin pillars of metaphysics and its cure, so his belief in hell bore almost no resemblance to that of a Catholic from the counter-reformation.

At times he couldn't believe it at all; he couldn't even *imagine* that his spinning his prayer wheel, his reciting the sutras, ever had released souls in any of the sixteen infernal chasms yawning beneath him. At other times still, especially when feverish, he thought in *very* concrete terms of hell, but not always, and not necessarily. At least for the purpose of entertaining an interesting conversation, he preferred stating that prayer primarily liberates the fettered mind; that enlightenment is the paradoxical prize one obtains for willingly sacrificing one's own enlightenment for that of another. Hence limitless compassion was rather like the bridge one must cross to reach the other shore. His favourite Chinese phrase for that virtue was *daci dabei*: big kindness, big sorrow; he'd always found the asyndeton striking.

"But for some reason," he told his guru with whom he met in the middle of the night, "I can't offer my peace for theirs. I think I'm straying from the big path; I'd prefer to follow a smaller track, to be saved by insight alone. I can't even play with the thought of burning for the sake of others."

"Why not?" asked the guru, careful not to inflate his ego by admitting that this kind of reluctance would make him *holier faster*. That is the kind of thing your guru would never admit. Perhaps, he suspected that Sanjo already had estimated the depth of the abyss and that that was why he feared crossing it. This guru would in any case never convince a disciple who shudders at his own insightfulness to continue to stagger along the path of wisdom. But perhaps he should.

"Because of the *fire!*" Sanjo answered. "I know it isn't real, but since I've only ever known imaginary fire, it seems real enough to me."

"What do you, then, make of the sutra of Ksitigarbha?" his guru asked him, and when he didn't reply, he added, "*Wo bu xia diyu, shui xia diyu* (我不下地狱，谁下地狱) …?" – "*If I don't descend into hell, who will…?*"

"Oh, I hate it. It's an entirely Chinese invention. But salvation isn't a social event."

"I think, perhaps, you'd prefer a worldly career," said his guru, and smiled, benevolently.

"You mean self-immolation?"

Forbidden by the lama, as well as by the authorities, to advise such a thing, the old man frowned at Sanjo's caustic remark, "Of course not. I was going to give you my blessing, but perhaps, on second thoughts, I shouldn't. Lest you hurt yourself."

"I'm so afraid of burning; you need not fear for me."

"*I* am free from fear," lied the old man, and gave him a book – *The Songs of Chu*. Subsequently, Sanjo memorized it. Otherwise he hadn't been very fond of Chinese poetry.

She was relieved to learn that poetry, to him, ultimately meant little more than allegiance to an old master. She dimly wanted him to take her, although not this night, and that would be impossible, if he proved too much of a poet.

Upon leaving the highlands, he had become a prizefighter. And that night, he had earned Electra just the amount of Hong Kong dollars she still needed to purchase a Black Star pistol. Electra melted in his embrace, quite like the sculptures of butter that had been on display in the temple; he brushed this association aside, because she was beautiful, having some of the allure of skilled transvestites. Perhaps she was indeed one, because he couldn't make her take the leather skirt off, but he cared little for that, since her mouth was so divine.

Menstruating, Electra thought, was letting go of a claim to existence. It was a study in loss. As the minuscule egg flowed out, it drained her of her most feverish ambitions. Electra, by nature, aspired to *glory*; she believed in it more than Sanjo had ever believed in hell. There were two kinds of glory: martyrdom and its inverse. As the mucous blood left her uterus, so did her aspiration to martyrdom. Now she only wanted to kill. She was thankful for that, but she didn't want to sleep with Sanjo like this, not for the first time, even if that meant Sanjo would take her for a man. She thought there would be an occasion for her to disprove his assumption later.

*

I was nothing like Electra.

I was traumatized by an almost trapezoid nose, eyes like cuts that never exhibited their whites, and many other features that betrayed my non-whiteness; and for some uncanny reason, I condemned heredity; I (subconsciously, of course!) thought being white should be conferred upon you quite like any other distinction; in the veinous temples of the most diaphanous white girls, I saw but filamentous medallions.

Crippled by ugliness, succumbing under the burden of imperfection, I had at last found David's plastic surgery clinic – this filthy fifth column of medical science; he was not only a surgeon, not only a most talented taxidermist, but a therapeutic genius. Oh, he was so eloquent that he made me doubt my inborn suspicion that other human beings were but automata – rants of this calibre could hardly be run by a programme, I thought. No machine would be capable of producing such megalomanic bile. His wasn't the kind of lowly intelligence that paves humanity's way to long, and surely destitute stars, no – he could *converse*! He impressed us. He couldn't relate some trivial piece of scientific news without revealing the statistical method that had wrought it; in mistaking everyone for idiots he was certain he seemed excessively smart. Apart from silicon, he implanted the seed of his learning in the women he operated on; a flabby particle of superiority was forever inserted into their hearts!

His life was the incremental process whereby his phantasies became more gross, and his need for vengeance more petty, more demanding.

I regret everything I just called him; I do – but what are you supposed to think of a man who doesn't woo you until you're anesthetized, groggy and bendable as hell; who takes you home and leads you through an endless marble corridor from the walls of which walls loom trophy after trophy: black rhinoceros; Asiatic cheetah; sea turtle; hippopotamus; crocodile; gorilla; elephant; deer…

After my seventh operation, and n-th molestation, he had brought me to his mansion. Wife and children were in Myanmar, or as he preferred to call it, Burma.

"I'm a prize hunter, that's why you're here," he explained, and all the near-extinct beasts nodded.

"Oh, don't cry," he said.

"You can't comfort me: you don't understand," I protested.

I felt dizzy: I wanted to escape from this honeycomb of dismembered glory, this prison of stolen pride, but I feared I couldn't; I feared it was not really this lazy rapist, draped in the skin of more ferocious males, who terrified me, I feared I wasn't trapped in his home so much as in my own very humanity....

"Don't be silly," he said. "We live no longer – alas – in the 19th century: don't you think every whore I ever brought here reacted just like you? You really think you're something, don't you? Why, I'll tell you: *all* of them faint, *all* of them bemoan the fate of these sorry creatures; *all* of them weep – yes, yes, I know what you're thinking – that otherwise I couldn't get an erection, well, I guess I'm a lucky man – *all* of them cry, and yet *none* are sentimental. They cry, because in killing the most spectacular specimen, I sever that great chain of selection that as of late has become the religion of the populace... What do you call it, now again? Something allegedly *clitelial* for development? Evulvution?

But don't you see – macroevolution is a finished chapter in the book of creation! They no longer develop anyhow, it only worsens the situation a *trifle* if I prematurely snatch them out of their vicious propagation cycle, like a *deus ex machina* assuring an apotheosis, stealing them away from *all this filth*," – he said, and clutched at my cleavage – "don't you see? As long as our industry and infrastructure infringe on their habitats, as long as we ascertain which ratio of predators and prey to maintain, as long as we drill the shit out of the Arctics, do you really think that *Darwinism* is operative? In my country, they import wolves in helicopters, and still the incestuous devils won't last for long: there's no natural selection at all: selection has become a matter of culture. Or don't you think I would have used a condom otherwise?"

*

On our way to his bedroom, in an octagonal parlour, we chanced upon what had been the *last wild Indochinese tiger,* Nero. The species had been considered practically extinct for years, and as all know, but few admit, it means little to the species itself whether there be two or six or forty individuals left, although it means the world to its sentimental killers. For us, spotting Nero pacing inaudibly through the tropical forest, had meant so much; the nine billion who had, more or less unwittingly, plotted against him, whether they had craved for the therapeutic benefits of his crushed bones or through sheer indifference watched on as sea levels were rising, all teared up as soon as he entered the stage of wild life protection. No tiger had ever been more beautiful, no animal had ever exuded more invincibility; no-one dared reveal to Nero that he no longer occupied the top of the food chain, that he in vain roamed the rainforest on the hunt for a female that wasn't his sister. That not even a sister was likely to be found in the crumbling wilderness. No-one dared tell him that he was a relic, enshrined in human compassion – which is always enkindled too late. The sensuality of hindsight and shame: humans revelled in such states of mind, whereas pre-emptive action bored them endlessly. Stubbornly, they let all but the mosquitoes die out, in order to, for ages, voluptuously mourn what they had wrecked; that was why they for so long had connived at the death of nature. They wanted to preserve wildlife forever in the alcoholic liquid of regret.

One day, Nero killed two poor poachers. In spite of all the surveillance cameras, the killing was not caught on tape; but Nero's microchip clearly gave him away. The only injuries the corpses had were deep scratches on their backs; he had not even tasted their flesh! The whole world watched, amazed. No-one, not even the families of the criminals, blamed Nero, although only heartless teenagers exhibited their joy publicly. Of course a human life was worth more than a tiger's, than the lives of ten thousand tigers, more than the life of the species itself – and yet, Nero didn't know this. The blasts of hot air hit his face; drops were threaded on his whiskers; in his emerald eyes the blood took on a brownish hue. His movements were as supple as if his body were made of water. He lived in paradise.

A few weeks later, I read in the papers that a doctor, who had opened a clinic in Hong Kong, had killed him, but I would never have called David a *doctor*. Since a hunter had lured him out, for David to shoot him right between the eyes, David was not legally at fault. Even if he had ventured to shoot him in his asylum, David would still not be incarcerated, or executed, for his sport; he could always pay for it. He had bought the death of the heir of all wilderness; the last subhuman claimant of greatness was dead, too dumb to sidestep a shot, although he surely wasn't too slow. Although tradition had it that Nero's carcass had unheard-of medicinal virtues, David didn't bother to make another fortune of his opponent; he had no such need.

Here he was, the last Indochinese tiger, perhaps the very last tiger, perhaps the last creature we instinctively feared. From now on our conceit would know no boundaries.

In spite of David's talent as a taxidermist, Nero looked awful. A monster summoned from some bestiary; the figment of a boyish imagination; pieces randomly assembled by a senile paleontologist. I found myself thinking: *This creature never existed anyway,* and instantly came to realize why the extinction of all inhuman animal life seems so dryly businesslike and so desperate at once: once they're dead, they really are dead. They never had "another shore": *this shore* was theirs, and once it was inundated, they drowned in silence. The victim is brutish and dumb, and the perpetrator is so talkative, he ...

"Meet my bodyguard," David said, and an almost grey, leonine man emerged from the corner. "He used to be a boxer: isn't he fine?" David asked, and his eyes flared as if he wanted to preserve the tall man, with the well-defined biceps of the most pious Tibetan monks, and place him on all fours, next to the tiger.

"Why..." I began.

"I receive so many angry letters, so many threats," said David and laughed. "Of course I don't take them seriously, because they don't have the wherewithal to hurt me. They're too poor to avenge this pretty monster," he said, and patted his giant cat. "But still, you see, my wife worries, so I hired this guy, who won the local tournament last week."

I had not really asked why he'd hired a bodyguard, but why *this man* had agreed to protect him. His pupils seemed burning hot; I could only withstand their gaze for a short moment. Then I looked down, and as I saw the Indian carpet, with a motif from the Upanishads, one bird gazing at a fruit that another bird devours, I realized why the stranger had agreed to this arrangement. *He was afraid of his compassion for the beast.* He knew this sorrow was not a quirk, or some misplaced paternal instinct; he knew that this compassion was an all-consuming fire, in which his self would be burned to ashes. Oh, away with you, compassion for all victims of empty gestures, pain at the sight of a senselessly humiliated nature! Compassion: be gone! Sanjo's erstwhile teacher had taught him that once ignited this flame will stop at nothing: there will be no more vanity, no more industries built on shaky confidences; there will be no more injustice, no more profit at the cost of life, there will be almost no more life – human life, as we know it, will be burnt to the ground: compassion will provide the final knock-out blow, and biting the dust at this almighty fighter's feet, humanity will at last find her purpose. And he was afraid of all of this, although it was so unlikely, and who wouldn't be? I stepped back.

"Prepare us some drinks, will you?" David said – because he loved to demand favours of his subordinates that clashed with the ones they were employed for. Sanjo said nothing, and left the room. Meanwhile I hurried to the porch, where Electra was hiding. She had slipped in through the gate as David and I made out in the car. I gave her his coordinates, entered the parlour and wisely seated myself at a divan at some distance away from the surgeon. David was cuddling the carcass, euphorically bragging about how we were to leave this planet all blown to smithereens, and find new virginal homes. Then Electra entered.

I never thought that Sanjo would take the bullet but he did. Bleeding, he was still as precious and detached as a ton of confiscated ivory, set alight by the authorities, burning to the end.

How often had Electra pondered why her heart should not race at the prospect of the elevation or fall of *her* person? Too often. There were so many individuals in the world – why could she not rejoice in *their* glory instead, and quiver at their pain? Often enough, she had shed the skin of personality that her feelings were unjustly wrapped in, and instead they had roamed freely, on the hunt for any valid excuse. She had so much compassion, not to say pity, that she could let loose whenever she wished to; her pity couldn't be confined to the life of Electra Ng, to her thievish passions, to her confused fears.... So in spite of it all, she did not pity her lover, all meekness and force, as supple as a tiger, and as shy: that would have been too easy; she pitied David. That he would have to witness, again, the wasting away of life, and all this lethally wounded nobility spread over the Indian carpet. Sanjo then mumbled something I couldn't hear.

"Yes, honey, you are," Electra said, "you're the greatest of all times."

And in concocting this lie, she was no better than Sanjo, who had acquiesced in being ruled even by this little piece of walking greed, this materialised sinful ignorance of what really mattered, this living syllogism proving the rottenness of the human race. She was no better than him, who had agreed to be the slave of cruelty just to escape from the flames of compassion.

孝思不匮 *(Xiaosi bu kui)*
ETERNAL FILIATION

I've done something terrible. There's nowhere for me to go but to my father's place. He lives in a suburb southwest of Stockholm, where all houses are alike, and merge into one another – even the trees are the same.... Only immigrants and a few bohemians live there: no-one will recognize me.

His place is a few steps away from the subway station – you follow the tracks and bear to the left; the flight lines converge at a point placed at a horizon so logical that one can't push forward in their direction.

At the arrival of the train, the snow sets off – crisp clouds of coldness evaporate in the alert winter atmosphere. I pierce them in order to reach my father's house, situated at the heart of a complex of peers: for a while, I'm at a loss, then I single it out: it's been thirteen years since I paid him a visit. It's still there, this livid, almost communist building with slender, squinting windows.

Loudly lamenting, the elevator carries me all the way to the fifth floor. There it is, again to the left, the door to his apartment. The extreme, near-disconcerting filth of the doormat. A great, golden 福 character against a red crinkled background hangs upside-down on the door. Suddenly, I no longer wish to enter.

For my grandfather to grant his wish of leaving the country, my father had to kneel before him, his hands on his thighs, his gaze fixed on the ground. He had to bang his forehead against the tiles. My grandfather supposedly became insensitive to other, less extreme, appeals, after he lost "everything" in the land reform campaigns. He'd been a factory-owner, and almost rich. The local committee had presented him with the choice to work in his own factory, heckled by his former subordinates, or to settle for a fraction of his land, and cultivate it on his own. He chose the latter, but he was inexperienced in the art of agriculture; because of his presumption, our family was ruined.

Crushed by this recent past that inextricably linked me to such strange and foreign events, I never listened to my father when he spoke – yet I know that the principal reason for my grandfather's stubbornness wasn't sentimental or patriotic. No. If he let go of his son, the family would in my father lose the most promising heir to its secret techniques, jealously propagated by lineage alone. Techniques at once martial and medical: strategies mobilized by the outraged pride of a nation whose war machine had turned out to be comparatively weak; alchemic dreams of a corporeal bliss during which the feet become Purling Sources, the stomach a Cinnabar Field, a point on the wrist the Gateway of Spirit, the top of the head the Assembly Point of a Hundred Rendezvous, the throat the Window of Heaven.... But in order to appropriate these sometimes dangerous techniques, one had to exercise – it was a salvation bought not by grace but by sweat. My father had escaped from the country on condition that he must always persevere in these exercises – and he'd kept his promise.

After my parents' divorce I initially stayed with him every other week. The small room facing the station was mine. The dirty window trembled in the gusts from trains that poured by like mercury; orange lights flowed in, filtered by the evermore grainy glasses of my unwashed window. The suburban stillness – so different from the centre, set a-whirl by life, where each friendship, each handshake, meant something reassuring. The city centre is small, and shrinking. My father has hardly seen it, although he's lived in Stockholm for decades; he knows he would harvest nothing there.

I slept poorly at his place, because I knew he'd wake me up at about 3:15am.

First, he'd reproach me – *"Yi dianr ye bu xiang nanzi han"* – that I didn't in the least possess the minimum of heroism necessary for a man. I retreated before this enormous charge, this burden consisting in the myth of spiritual greatness... *"Bu neng chi ku de nanzi han meiyong"*: *boys unwilling to endure suffering are useless* – to "endure", in Chinese, is tantamount to *eat* the bitterness of life. After half an hour of lessons I could hardly grasp, we would "exercise" *(duanlian shenti)*. I wasn't expected to abandon my standing position before my knees would drum against one another, before my arms would tremble like the members of a marionette – or else, an even more absurd harangue would follow.

How silly it was! I had not yet turned fourteen when I revolted against it all, but not in the way in which young minds dulled by desperation revolt. I was rather cold-blooded. My mother worked for the social services – maybe that was why I was already quite insightful when it came to the mechanisms regulating Swedish society. I awaited an opportunity – and it came. In order to relieve my fever, my father treated me with acupuncture. The marks left by the needles were hardly visible. I asked if the *cups* could be used for my discomfort and, blinded by my curiosity, he placed a few on my back. It was nice; I fell asleep, and when I woke up I felt perfectly at ease. Nonetheless, the cups had left horrible bruises, quite like the fingerprints of enormous cephalopods. Before they faded, I turned to the *skolkurator* for help, a sycophant of the social services, who worked at our school under the guise of a therapist. She was a huge woman who seemed to unfold from her crotch like a tent on its pole.

I complained of my father's severity, and she was already willing to appeal to the authorities *(Socialtjänsten)* when I laid bare the bruises, those irrefutable proofs of his perversity, as if I had wanted to underline my words with a blinding trace. She almost fainted. In Sweden, it's illegal to give children certain TCM treatments, as my father must have known. My mother had conscientiously explained all blunders he shouldn't commit – in accomplishing them, one after another, it was as if he'd followed this list. Tired of his presumptuous ignorance, my mother, who knew he wasn't excessively cruel, allowed the whole affair to unfold, which, once launched, would not stop until it had separated, by injunction, a father from his child. This bureaucratic apparatus cut to the quick. It's a superstitious machinery: the slightest harshness is sufficient to erect an official abyss between the generations.

During the meetings with the case workers, he didn't look at me – and I felt no shame, spurred on as I was by the despotic compassion of which I was the victim. Compassion had rendered me a monster of comfort, or, in a word, Swedish; I had acquired an ugly and functional IKEA-soul.

"Is it correct that you oblige your son to do physical exercises each night?"

"..."

"Children need to sleep, to rest, you know."

Initially, he refused to answer them. Then, he spoke, his voice more coarse than ever, his accent unbearably embarrassing – the studied articulation I knew he had mastered so well, because I'd heard him recite poetry, was gone; from his mouth emerged only a deformed mass of noise in which all tones were drowned. He said, "*Träna också är vila*," – that even the exercises were, in fact, a kind of rest. The women from the social services gazed at each other.

"But I don't want to!" I exclaimed. "I don't want to – I don't believe in your stories! *He said that his master could fly!*" Even my mother looked at me with some contempt – these convictions at the bosom of the tradition from which I wished to escape weren't meant to be divulged before my father's judges.

They smiled. "Is it true?" they asked, ready to note his answer in the documents that were to belong to the dossier of my domestic suffering.

"No," he said. My mother exhaled in relief. Then he added, "It wasn't him, it was my master's master."

My mother feared that they would declare him insane. But in their eyes all foreigners have their proper share of insanity, and they could hardly fill our institutions with all of them.

He was immediately deprived of custody – in addition, a restraining order was issued. Thus we were torn apart. We saw each other rarely and never at his place.

I'm still sitting in the stairwell when I hear the elevator ascending: I know who it is. I get up to greet him: I find it difficult to look him in the eyes.

"You've done something terrible," he says. I shrug my shoulders, preparing to reveal it to him, but he interrupts me, "I don't want to know anything about it. *Haohan zuo shi haohan dang"* – *the hero deals with the consequences of his actions.* "Hero" here signifies neither the main character in some fictive work nor someone whose soul overflows with outdated virtues: it has nothing to do with a profusion of virtues. It signifies nothing spectacular. It's the measure of a Chinese boy, in particular when you scold him for not living up to it. In vain, I would have told him that I don't *feel* Chinese, because one of the characters in my name is, in fact, 汉 : *han.* But I go by my Swedish name: I've never availed myself of the one he chose for me. I can hardly pronounce it.

"If you want to stay with me, you'll have to live like me. Otherwise you should leave now."

I stay.

Indoors, everything is as before. Everything is just as I left it. The elevator still resounds in the near-empty rooms: I shudder as I hear its strange, plaintive echo. Perhaps it has become even more disagreeable: the dissonance of an inarticulable pain. No decoration on the walls. Here and there, Chinese antiquities powdered with dust. The same layer of grease covers all surfaces in the kitchen; the same silverfish inhabit the bathroom; the same palimpsests of grammar lessons on ruled sheets show how little progress he's made in learning my mother tongue since I moved out, and – my bed is still there. Without sheets, a naked bed. He brews tea, and serves me slices of fruit, and it is only then that I realize that he's pleased that I've returned.

"From now on, you have to start over. It's late, but it isn't too late." We sit on the brown leather sofa. The nice, sunny weather outdoors is concealed behind the thick curtains. His place isn't even in poor taste: no taste at all rules here.

I start over.

After the exercises, he sings, perhaps out of joy, and sometimes he plays what looks quite like a harp as well – it's called "guzheng" I believe, and he plays it like someone who has always been alone.

Yet, he has proselytes who idolize him. They often come over in the evenings. Each time, he cooks. The sweet odour of boiling rice pierced by the rays of sharper fragrances: Sichuan pepper, ginger, garlic, vinegar. The infinite registers of the five tastes combine in sublime compositions, unheard-of and ravishing.... I discover that eating à la chinoise is a pleasure much more variegated and spiritual than sex. Maybe I'm sensitive just because I think I'm safe, but I find that the food is so tonic that eating it is quite like crying. Sometimes the meal is suspended, for him to demonstrate his tricks on his students. They always end up sinking to the ground. I ask myself whether these defeats are polite concessions, or if he really, improbably, triumphs by force. Perhaps the truth of the matter somehow contains both these extreme possibilities. Perhaps one mustn't choose at all.

Slowly, the amused horror in the eyes of his novices begins to convince me of the legendary superiority that I've always considered a fraud. But I won't penetrate into this mystery: for now we hear the doorbell ring – an anguished metallic sound as from a whipped machine. I know who they are. They've come to get me.

The chain is broken. The frail thread of tradition has snapped – no-one will propel it further, it ends here. The exercises would disgust my sons, if I could have learnt them myself, as they've always disgusted me – my sons too will be weak by choice, they too will be swine. There will be no more art propagated by filiation alone; filiation simply isn't enough for art.

Our eyes no longer meet. For the first time in my life, I feel the need to bend my knees and hit my forehead against the floor, by chance just before his plastic pink slippers. Yet I cannot, not since my arms are now crossed behind my back, but because I am fettered by my own show of indifference, infected by a boreal dignity from which I will never recover. *Even if it does not show, father, in my heart I easily extract myself from their grip, and I throw myself from the window to float along the façade, carried by the wings of the invisible bird that is your dying secret.*

ORA ET LABORA

Fostered as I was in the altruistic parochialism that reigns on the borders of nature reserves, I could not but acknowledge the beauty of these old rock formations, worn smooth by the regular slaps of the sea, rocks plunged in a fluid flogging, eternal footstools of fickle herons. I stood at the shore of Kosterhavet; the wind had abated, the tattered clouds floated slowly above me, beneath me age-old Bohus-granite blushed as the oblique rays of a sinking sun hit it, and, like a benevolent god, I too found it to be *good*. Kosterhavet is the sole marine national park in Sweden; on one of the islands moored in this sanctified water my mother had inherited her parents' country seat. Even before I was born, my grandparents had transformed the property into a recreational centre, where meditation classes, workshops in mostly oriental spirituality and general health and wellness training were held. My mother had cultivated this sprawling tradition, and she regularly hosted courses and events in her childhood home, although we lived in the capital. During the long summer vacations I always accompanied her there; half-heartedly trying diaphragmatic breathing, focussing the third eye on my brow, or the "cinnabar field" beneath my belly button, depending on the content of the course then offered. But I was thirteen that year, and only reluctantly left the city. I feared that in my absence, my lies would be debunked; I feared that what little respect I had gained in the eyes of my peers through the fever of my imagination – with which I always tried to forestall their predetermined disappointment at my weakness, that what little acceptance I had earned through wanton obedience and flattery, would evaporate, and be gone when I returned. So I had pithily protested at our seasonal installation at this last stronghold of aquatic manifoldness – and in the car, I had cried in my pillow; a low but frittering sound remindful of the whimsical warble of small birds. My mother never heeded high-pitched arguments, and nothing could be gained by crying out loud.

Yet I had been brought up on the conviction that the sea water was nowhere else as pure as in this little sea, and I could not, for all my adolescent discontent, deny the beauty of the gneissic banding on the rocks, or the incredible freshness of an air in which you could taste the salt. At last, I was happy I had been dragged along. Bitterly satisfied by beauty, I returned to the house.

Because of the muted tantrum I had thrown in the car, my mother had allotted me a room of my own: the attic in the reconstructed barn. Usually guests were housed there, but now it was mine. The ground floor served as "Meditation Hall", with parqueted flooring and many different species of candlesticks, cushions and small stools in styrofoam, sometimes slightly warped, shaped by the buttocks of a long series of visiting navel-gazers…. Right at the entrance stood an untuned piano, on which I sometimes, at night, played with my miserable small hands, engineered to grip objects less extended than a seventh chord….

That summer my mother had recruited a factotum of sorts: a young man equally well-equipped to fix the blocked pipes in the shower-room, to renovate our garden sheds, and to enkindle the tea lights in the sauna. To curtail expenditures, she had hired only one man for all practical work. He dwelled in his own caravan on the lawn: apart from himself, it contained only what could be expected: bottles of liquor, knives and books read too greedily, too many times. Whenever my mother ordained him to perform some, to my childish sensitivity, demeaning chore – such as driving to the convenience store for tampons, or picking up a belated guest at the railway station – I blushed. His eyes, so light as to appear diaphanous, his tattooed hands, his bony, always bare feet, and above all his stubborn silence implied that only the most strenuous assignments could satisfy his craving for lactic acid, an almost mystical need for the kind of physical pain that alone enforces a masculine identity.

I lay in my bedstead recess, and witnessed the ice blue shade of the mint green cupboard doors basking in moonlight. Although I had a small kitchen, complete with a sink and taps from which our allegedly salubrious well-water flowed, there was no toilet in my attic; the closest ones were on the other side of the lawn. I had to walk past the stunted apple trees, some tarnished brass statues, and of course, the egg of his caravan, seemingly swelling with obscure nightly activities, shrouded in the mist of his impenetrable dreams. Early that summer I noticed that when I went out in the garden late at night, two delusions often followed each other in such a way that I had the impression that my life conformed to the symbolic law of dreams rather than to the natural laws of reality. *One* reverie can easily pass any cost-benefit test: it may spur you on, it may instill in you the small but ever imprecise quantity of rationally unjustifiable pride required for most worthwhile successes, or it may offer a clue as to why you should go on living, in spite of all. But when delusions follow one another in the way events succeed each other in my dreams, something good rarely comes of it. Most often, nothing comes of it but a sense of eerie disorientation.

Late at night it was. As I stepped out, barefoot, on the wet grass, in the lush summer darkness, the first fantasy laid hold of me: I abashedly hoped that *he* would emerge from his white shell, like a newly hatched incarnation of all my own youthfully vague carnal desire, drag me away and cover me with the butterflies and flowers carved in his skin. I knew that dreaming of this was tantamount to wishing for an everlasting separation, because my mother would sooner rather than later find out about it, and fire him; she had probably already seen the precocious and silly longing that was then the thorn in the back of my nights.

I knew that he was more – that he must be more – than the humiliated worker of my nightmares, that there was more to his life – much more – than the hand-to-mouth existence I observed, and the wasted perfection of his body. I knew it was not that simple, and that somewhere behind his irresistibility, there was a soul, or something like that – I knew that he, like me, cocooned himself in an inner life that had little to do with what I admired in him, and yet I wished for all the humiliation that I imagined on his behalf – and which he in all likelihood never sensed at all, to transmute into a rage, in which he would rape me by the blackcurrant bush. This fantasy lasted for as long as I staggered about outdoors, and there was, admittedly, nothing very delusional about it; a figment of my imagination had short-circuited my empathy, and I felt nothing for him but violent longing.

But this harmless fantasy somehow led to another, in which I escalated the stairs back to my room, quite as I matter-of-factly did, groped at the doorknob (placed at a different height from what I was used to), lifted the sheets and as I prepared to slip in between them, back into the spot still heated by my body's warmth, discovered that *I* was already in bed.... And in my drowsily dazed state, I could without difficulty feel the silky softness of my thighs, and the tenseness of my entire body, dressed in a pair of briefs and a tank top at best, this frail body harbouring a desire which it could not contain – a desire which at times even contemptuously left its fretting shell, to wander alone in the garden and along the shrinking shore.

THE FOUNDLING

She'd felt him hit her cervix for a year, and yet he hadn't reached high enough for something to come to life. He dreamt that he penetrated so deep into her as to finally emerge from her mouth, becoming a word solemnly pronounced by her: not even in his dreams could he impregnate her, he just passed straight through. She dreamt that she was cut in half, that sex and mouth were rejoined in an orifice more sincere than either had been, and that this still wasn't enough. An ever chaste interiority mocked their awkward attempts at unification. The kernel of life was ungraspable, even for the farthest-reaching of lovers: they agreed that it was lodged too deeply, or perhaps too shallowly; in any case, it remained hidden, in spite of their furrowing, and their cells didn't fuse.

He became fond of saying that her womb was as barren as her joints were pliable, but he was now in his mid-thirties, and his friends – the very friends who'd envied him for having Dolly, had babies now, and couldn't afford to listen to this nonsense. *They* wouldn't give up their family-lines for any half-acrobatic sport in the world, they said. At the end of the day, genetic survival mattered more to them than the kind of orgasms that can make you faint. It mattered most of all, they said.

Dolly, exceedingly flexible, blamed his uselessness on his constant smoking.

In a city located at the bottom of a basin, low below sea level, they rented a small apartment and decided to "live" there. But eight years before renting this mouldy home with its stale air and ageless, "functional" furniture, they had met *elsewhere*.

She no longer expected much of Hector. She wanted only to shield him from his own mediocrity. With his small, balding head and large hands he looked like a sailor from a revolutionary poster. She knew that his brain was charged with doubts that overwhelmed it, doubts it could never resolve. She knew that it dreamt of righteousness, of binding righteousness; of a world where all would be abreast of each other, because only one unmentionable force would be above them.

To dissipate his thoughts, she suggested that they visit the winter market.

Now, they're there.

As always when they're out together, she feels a bit unreal. When they just go on living the parallel lives of life-long partners who rarely infringe on each other's territories, she's fine. But whenever they try to spend some time together, the two of them, whenever that's the articulated purpose of their activity, she feels as if she's made up.

Especially now.

Because, ever since they left the crowd in the midst of which the juggler whirled a burning rope around his neck, Hector has been *different*. It was a long time since she had seen him in such high spirits. When he holds her shoulder, she feels his heart beat against it, with childish expectation; she didn't know that he was susceptible to this kind of holiday exhilaration. They pass a church decorated with illuminated snowflakes; on the square next to it there're striped awnings everywhere, the wind impatiently jerks at them. He checks her pace at each stand, and sometimes puts a piece of cheese in her mouth, sometimes a laced olive, sometimes a plastic spoon charged with marmalade. He even raises the paper cup with *glogg* to her lips; he's so fumbling that the sweet and sticky liquid trickles along her chin – but he dismisses her protests with a laugh. He drags her along; he does not spare her from a single taste, whether it be snails, preserved ginger, sweet-scented wine, hot chestnuts or candies. At the merry-go-round, he cuts into the line before a family with small children. At its revolving, screeching disc stand:

- a very small space rocket of iron sheets which rather reminds one of a vertical incubator;
- the skeleton of a dinosaur;
- an ostrich;
- and a falcon with its wing tips still dripping of blood

– and they all carry gleaming cuirasses in red, green and gold, and small cages for the children to sit in. The conductor explains to two brothers that only one child can ride each aching beast, but as he addresses them, he entreatingly stretches his hands out against Hector: Dolly he doesn't even look at. Yet she smiles apologetically; she's always well-behaved, she possesses a kind of ever dismal tact. If Hector were to straddle the dinosaur, he would break its spine; the structure wouldn't hold. The children that merrily go round are all less than fourteen years old. Hector and Dolly leave these crumbling riding animals to continue indefinitely on their circular track, as the melody fades away in the noise. "Drink", he says, and she obeys, because she's *happy*.

Is this only the mild intoxication, or is it his recovery, is it the much-longed for oblivion? After eight years, she had scaled the wall of paradise and come to live with him, but at the airport she no longer recognized him. Perhaps his unrecognizability is only chemical – because, ever since it was found that he did not share the short-sightedness we call sanity, he has been drugged. And when she came to see him, his misanthropy – which had been so uplifting, and so full of transhuman hope when they first met – now weighed heavily on him. But at long last, he follows no longer the ordinations; he swallows no pyschoanaleptics; the untouched charts with pills pile themselves in drifts in the cupboard, insinuating the looming possibility of an overdose. Dolly isn't opposed to that, as long as he, once, before the final exaggeration, just momentarily becomes himself again.

But now, when he humiliates himself at the Christmas market, on the square where the rectangular fountain has been covered to give room for more commercially ritual spectacles, when he surmounts his disgust and melts into the swarming crowd, elbows his way in the drink-line, and feeds her with the same fanatical tenderness that sailors formerly thought the pelican lavished on its young – it crosses her mind that perhaps the ordeal is over. Perhaps he has returned to life and to the living that are its captives.

But if he, as the doctors expect, is to attempt suicide, this erratic baby, so fumbling and violent, so lonely in the throngs, then she wishes that he would indeed succeed, and take his contagious stupidity with him to the grave. *Hector!* – Dolly thinks – life *can't be lost: life is its own loss; it loses itself, little by little; it drowns giggling in its own reflexion – heroically, it raises still a sinking fist from the quagmire.*

But ever since they passed the juggler with a burning snare, his old overweening pain has vanished: with disturbing humility he absorbs all pleasures the market has to offer – perhaps he's just a little too greedy, a little too cynical – but that doesn't bother Dolly. He always used to be like that, before his breakdown, it's only his old fever, resurgent after a long rest. He hurts the candyfloss-seller by refusing to accept the change; the latter brandishes the bills as if to menace them, a gesture that states, "No charity, please!"

She loses sight of him for just a moment, and then ... In these tangled masses, in which Hector despises all who indulge in pleasures he either declares to be nil or theatrically embraces, he's suddenly anchored. He's no longer adrift, he dances no longer to the hydra's tune – he bends his large back; he crouches down as if he folded a pair of giant wings – he abstains even from the euphoria that he must feign in order to approach other men on an equal footing, and all this takes place before she catches up with them; in her absence, he has become *two*. A boy, perhaps one decimeter shorter than her, has joined them; Hector bends down as if to inhale the warmth of his breath; it was long since he bowed like that before *her*. Perceiving her presence, Hector turns around and presents her to the boy, to whom he gives an impenetrable look, as expressionless as a hermetically closed bivalve. The boy clears his throat.

"He wants fifty cents for the merry-go-round," Hector explains. The boy wears a grey fleece jacket, outgrown jeans, ending high above his ankles, no socks, and mud-stained sneakers. A conditioned reflex makes her go through her wallet, but Hector stops her hand midway to the boy's outstretched palm: it's suspended there, since he doesn't loosen his grip. The boy knits his thick brows, beneath which his high eyelids arch, marbled by veins in which the blood floats so close to the surface as if it strove to absorb oxygen directly from the air, without the mediation of his heart....

These eyes are almost on the same level as hers; she isn't tall and usually wears high heels – if only the orthopedist hadn't told her that her Achilles' tendons would be permanently shortened as a result, she would have worn them tonight – now, they're almost equally tall, and yet she stands before him, with her hand locked in Hector's grip on its way to his, caught in this silly and haughty gesture; the coin between her index finger and thumb burns her skin through the glove....

She looks at Hector who in turn scrutinizes the boy. He says, "Aren't you too big for the merry-go-round?" The boy doesn't answer, but lowers his eyes. He lowers them with the same dry submissiveness with which a wolf bares its throat – and a streak of the white of his eyes is still visible beneath the lids. She observes this blind splinter of the cornea, milky-white like opalescent absinth; it reminds her of the crushed ice from the fish-stand nearby, for it is as wet, cold and insensitive to the modesty of his eyelid as the ice-bed is to the death throes of the fish.... Only then does Hector let go of her hand. He studies the boy with the same inscrutable expression as before, and she awkwardly replaces the coin in her pocket. The shoulder-bag of a passer-by hits her in the back.

"Say it," Hector proposes, but the boy remains mute. She makes an effort to leave; since their arms are still intertwined, Hector as a result for an instant loses his equipoise; he gives her a newly awakened gaze, and then addresses the little stranger, "Come with us instead. We're going to the Ferris wheel. Ah, come, it's on me."

During the last few years, she has developed a certain oversensitivity to heights. She must have forgotten to tell him. It isn't really a phobia, for more often than not, she can enter the plane without difficulty, and keep her weakness in check till it lands again; only rarely does she need to inhale some extra oxygen in the airport sickroom before boarding. She loves to pierce the clouds – the clouds, saturated in fleeting pride, too soft to be alive, flesh compounded out of rain....

But on other occasions, she can't even take the escalator in a skyscraper without cold sweat dripping from the palms of her hands and down the small of her back. And sometimes, but rarely, she loses her head; it's like an eternally recurrent swoon, a stabbed consciousness interspersed with dark wounds; everything fuses before her eyes, and then she suddenly sees farther into the distance than ever – but her knees give way and her hands tremble like aspen leaves. Legend has it that the cross was carved from aspen wood, and that the tree still trembles at the enormity of its crime; it's the same wasting regret that chokes her, when she's afraid of heights. But it isn't that bad. And who knows when Hector will gain this kind of momentum next, who knows when she'll find his drained corpse in the shower cabin, or worse still, a note from him on the pillow, stating that he went away to fight in the last of unjust wars, the last and final war. Who is *she* to decline the whims of her resurrected lover? The boy, at least, is up for a ride. Arm-in-arm, with Hector in the middle, they walk up to the big wheel.

In the line she buys a Danish pastry and divides its eight in two zeros, asking the boy whether he wants a piece. To her surprise he doesn't take it until Hector tells him to. A silence ensues. The ride is three rounds long; not that much, she soothes herself. It's one of the highest wheels of Europe; the brand is called *Diamant*. On its giant hub there's a pentagon, perhaps the star of Bethlehem. The structure is white but illuminated with pink lights; the gondolas swing from their creaking attachments. From the speakers music flows, the lyrics seem to return to the topic of immortality, or something; she can't presently pay attention to them.

As she hands the ticket collector the three tickets, dark like holly leaves, the trembling of her fingers betrays her. A pungent stench of anxiety already emerges from her pores as they mount the gondola, which rocks in reaction to their weight. It rises quickly. Soon they have passed the obelisk where a verdigris angel balances. She bites her tongue until the taste of iron becomes unbearable. Her saliva is already too sweet.

"What's your name?" she asks, and then the entire universe fades away.

*

In this formlessness, she cannot see the present, the present smile of the boy, or his hair stirred by the wind. She can only see the past. She sees it clearly, and yet she doubts it.

*

She and Hector met on a boat crossing the English Channel. Then, he had been a newly arrived immigrant, fleeing a war in which factions fought over *his* country – but none of the factions were his; and he hadn't been called

Hector then, but had a much holier name. She was just a high-school student.

They were both leaning over the gunwale, but only she was writing on a napkin. She was writing furiously, and he knew she was composing a poem.

"Let me have a look," he said, although she was a stranger, and also a girl.

She refused.

He knew there would be rhyme in her poem, and that was why he wanted to read it. He hated poems without rhymes; they were like horses without hooves, he thought. He didn't doubt it would be a horrible poem, because she'd composed it in such fervour, but he *knew* it would have rhymes.

Rather than letting him read it, she threw it overboard; it couldn't even sink, it was too insubstantial:

Why do I love the sea,
The drunken sea,
so vividly?
Because of the firmness of her flight?
Because she carries heaven's weight?
Because her violence is so light?
Because of the mildness of her hate?
To love the sea – to love the flicker
of a mist that's growing thicker,
Sea, your broken patterns of cold foam
are vines that grow on crawling hills…
To love the fear a fluid eternity instills
into each rigid frame…
Ever-writhing, veinous grey, never healed,
stranded, lame,
O calmness, oceanic pain…
The waves that crush the drowning light
are the scales on muscles cramping
of a reptile shedding skin

— but here, there is no heart within.
The sea is in its very depth but extended skin.
Why do I love the tide, avenger of all human pride,
why do I love the sea, that once, without regret,
will collect what shall be left of me?
The sea, the devil's fan that grinds all bone to sand:
Why do I love the sea
the drunken sea
so vividly, so much?

"It's good you committed it to the waves," he said.

"I didn't," she said.

"I saw you did."

"That was another poem," she insisted.

Suddenly, they realized that they both liked littering up the sea.

He was quite a hypocrite and wouldn't bring this affinity to its logical conclusion until she reached the age of consent, two years later. Instead, he went on and on about how special she was, and she ...

*

After one revolution, she inhales deeply. It was only the novelty. Now she knows what awaits – she can no longer fear, she persuades herself. The machine takes off again; they are propelled upwards by this giant breaking-wheel, along which they crawl like insects. It spins so slowly, this wheel, and one hears how the wind howls in its hollow bones. Hector, who holds her hand, carefully puts it down in her lap, gets up and seats himself on the other side, next to the boy. The gondola sways at the shift, and again, everything loses edge.

*

For two years they stayed in touch over the internet, and then at last she came to see him in Belgium.

Like most men his size Hector was not at all cunning; there was no need for it.

He was a bit dull-witted, although not to the extent that he seemed, and liked when they begged for it. Dolly had to surmount all her pride to satisfy his inveterate laziness. He wiped off her face with his handkerchief and said, "There, there; say it again now."

She'd never begged before, and she believed that everything that went against the grain for her was some kind of necessary penance: thus she had expected this new-found desperation sooner or later to give rise to saintliness. It didn't.

"You've changed," he said.

"You mean, I look different," she suggested.

"That's not it."

And only then did she realize that no accusations, no allegations of manipulation, could compensate for her own guilt: she had lost it. That's not to say she had lost some fictitious membrane, although she'd lost that as well.

Whatever she had had at the age of fourteen was now lost, and perhaps she would not have lost it so irrevocably, had she not fallen for *him*. Not to say that he'd deprived her of her innocence, because his own by far surpassed hers; but in acknowledging her gift, he'd perverted it.

Her decay was patent, and never did she by this decay intend that her by now fuller pockets of fat had spoilt some hypothetical infantile charms, she didn't mean that her slowed-down gesticulation and metabolism had ruined her appeal. She knew that such superficial details couldn't have disappointed him, Hector, her first admirer.

What she'd lost was rather the conviction that one day love would, somehow, be elevated to a rule for all of humanity; she'd lost her god-given insight into the oneness of all. Formerly, she'd unlocked this truth from the profundities of nature; she'd been convinced of it to the point where she almost turned invisible, where her contours where almost absorbed by her surroundings. She'd *known* that there was nothing in the towering monuments which she didn't incapsulate in her heart. And suddenly she knew it no longer.

*

The second turn is over. Her nausea dissolves as they are at the level of the bay, and returns with metronomic regularity after the first quarter of the third round....

*

Hector knew that he had been too extravagant in his praises, and he knew he would have to pay the price for this. He also suspected the price would be a lifelong commitment. But when she came back, again two years later, the matter no longer interested him. He had, he said, outgrown the urge to worship, which had formerly made him so sensitive to all that was too frail to be conquered: and would she please forgive him?

He was by now ripe for war, or for peace, he said, and if he didn't make a difference now, he would never make one. At last, he realized that there was nothing infamous about being conquered: that was how he lost his former adoration for those he couldn't, for shame, exert any earthly influence over; children for example. Even war is good, he insisted, if both sides fight in earnest, that is, to defeat the opponent, and not to "save" him, and if he'd ever attempted to save her, would she forgive him this, as well?

He'd become a believer in revelation, or more precisely, in the chaotic character of revelation. The variegated, yet strangely unified, quality of religion, proved that its truth was manifested piecemeal, or even worse: that each revelation was unique; that the divine never assumed the same form twice, that it never enkindled the same bush twice, or forced intercourse with the same priestess – twice. God was always, in a word, unrecognizable, as unrecognizable as the *righteousness* of a foreign custom.

As unrecognizable as her original self was by now, the self that she'd thrown overboard. So that was the last vestige of his love for her: that he celebrated the triumph of the unrecognizable.

"I know they are wrong," he said, "to kill – but it *is* admirable to kill with your own hands, instead of using the expedient of a robotic slave.... I feel like sacrificing myself. I never felt like this before. I've felt like fighting ever since they declared the bombings 'bloodless': I feel like watching my blood flow just to prove them wrong. This urge is a denunciation: it denounces what we have believed in for so long – that responsibility can be spirited away through technology. I feel like assuming responsibility for death, for someone else's or my own."

He confided in her his broodings like this, and more – this vague subversiveness wasn't quite what she'd expected from the reunion of lovers after years apart.

He told her that soon he could bear their hypocrisy no longer, and then he would have to kill, if only to prove *them* right, if only to justify *their* tepidness, if only to prove that only the tepid deserve to wield power.

"For the sake of making a difference?" she asked, and he confirmed that.

"Perhaps," she said, "making a difference is something of the past. Perhaps leaving no trace at all is more glorious now."

"Is that why you chose me?" he asked. "Because you knew that I'd be forgotten in my lifetime, buried alive in history? Did you choose this nobody that I am to preserve your virginity?"

She suspected he was right, that that was why he'd chosen her, and she him: because in each other's company, they were still alone. No matter how close they grew, there was a screen between them, something like a mirror....

*

The ride is over. She retches as soon as she gets down on the platform. Hector does not come to her rescue, even though she pukes at the fake fur collar of her gauntlets, just a few threads – linear drops locked in a cold, lucid gel. But she doesn't blame him! She doesn't blame him, for now he focuses all his force on one sole point – and this enigmatic concentration is worth so much more than all her misgivings. Then he comes, she takes him by the arm, and together they walk homeward again. Sleet is falling; the crystals sparkle in the street lighting. She doesn't need to turn about to realize to whom the steps that follow them belong. He follows them all the way home, as persistent and unassailable as the core of life itself.

FRIEDA ROOS

My cousin Frieda Roos always complained about her childhood. No-one took her seriously. I had once witnessed the source of her discontent, yet I too trivialized it.

Her mother stood before her, arms akimbo, with her face strangely distorted. As if one of the strings that held her upright had been severed, she suddenly knelt before her daughter, theatrically disjointed. She slammed her head against the floor, then stood up, and exclaimed, "What does your highness want? Cry, cry, cry; and you can have anything!"

I have never heard anyone voice her sarcasm so loudly since. It was a deafening question.

She puckered her lips, made an almost graphic sound – the kind you expect to find only in speech bubbles, "Ugh!" and spat on the ground. Thereupon she resumed her fixed position with outstretched arms, only to kneel once more. She was careful to rub her forehead against the sputum on the ground. It was evident she announced some almost propositional meaning by this gesture, but I could not think of one. To be honest, I was petrified.

Meanwhile, Frieda was curled up in a corner of her bed, a creepily innocent one, draped in pink, taut sheets. Her face was livid. In her position, I would not have wept. But she howled, staring at her mother as if she were an apparition.

Not until Mrs Roos had left the room could I silence her.

"You saw," she said. Her voice did more than tremble: the intonation was, so to speak, convulsive.

At that time, I was only fourteen years old. Frieda was one year younger than me, yet taller. Presumably stronger as well. All her long, sinewy limbs were now awfully rigid, locked in the most unnatural way. Since I was only fourteen years old, and admired her so much, not *her* of course, but her body, this frame that some wild panic had temporarily wrecked, I did not ask myself what the mock kowtows had signified. I did not wonder whether her mother often repeated them, or if she sometimes paid her undue respects differently. I did not think about why she felt so exhilarated by her amalgamation of contradictory poses: first, she had knelt, then spat, then knelt again. I did not ask Frieda whether her mother relished in the profound disgust she clearly felt at the sight of her daughter, nor did I ask since when she had elevated this disgust to an almost ceremonial feature of their daily lives.

Instead, I slowly disentangled her arms. She pressed them violently to her chest, holding herself down in an awkward embrace. I had to put all my strength into this business. I undid the bundle she had become.

"You saw," she insisted.

I stroke her cheek and said, "I saw nothing."

*

In her position, I would not have wept. There are all sorts of tears. Hers were the kind that despair thrives on. I could not admonish her to feign indifference, she had to learn it on her own. But she seemed never to learn. Year after year she cut herself open, was sown, anesthetized, and sent back home in one piece, where she cut deeper – but, alas, never deep enough to exterminate the germ. One cannot blame her for slowly losing track of time, on all her countless journeys to the hospital.

At her worst, she resembled mostly an incoherent accusation, held together by the stitches.

Had her mother only occasionally vomited on the piano keyboard during family gatherings! Had she only once slapped her in public! Then there would have been witnesses. But now, there were none; no-one knew what strange rites her mother celebrated at her bedside. Or, for that matter, why.

*

Our mothers were sisters, mine the younger one. I always knew there was a world of difference between them, although I could never spell out wherein it consisted. Her parents were not better dressed, nor richer, nor more well-read than mine; but there was an incontestable, almost eerie supremacy in their way of acting. In hindsight I believe it was sorrow.

Our family visited theirs quite often; they never came to us. Their house was more spacious than ours and my aunt the superior hostess. It was midsummer and the fruit trees' boughs were festooned; the plates decked with rancid seafood.

Her parents exclaimed my name as I entered; Frieda's younger sister welcomed me in silence.

"You've grown," my aunt said.

"Where is Frieda?" I asked. When she was not present, I could not bother to be polite.

"In her room, I think," her mother responded, almost singingly. She had received an armful of flowers; nothing in her demeanor betrayed that Frieda had all but died two weeks ago, in yet another attempt at suicide.

I opened the door and found her standing on the threshold. We observed each other for a moment. It was as if I had opened a closet and looked into a mirror. Then she retreated and procured a dire file from her desk drawer.

"Just in case I die," she said. "Keep these for me."

"What is it?"

She blushed. "They're poems," she confessed.

I said that I did not want them, but she insisted.

She would not join us for dinner, although later on we picked flowers and wrought crowns out of them, twining metal thread into their gaudy tenderness. I was not ashamed of it, not even then. The sun did not set but lingered on, diffusing a most hesitant light on our long conversation.

"If, on this night, you place a selection of seven buds under your pillow, you will dream of someone who can kill you," I told her, unsure of how much she had gathered of Swedish culture, since her family had lived abroad for so long, but still eager to strike that special chord.

"I already know one," she said, and all the blood in my body recoiled back into my vanquished heart. A fluid, dreamy thrust! In comparison with it no later heartbeat has really deserved the name.

*

I did not find her poems till a couple of years afterwards. I was maybe sixteen by then and committed the error of bringing them to the boarding school where I was housed.

Frieda, for a girl your age, these poems are well-written; there is no denying that. But what do you mean by writing well, by writing *this* well at such a tender age? When did you last hear of a poem where rhythm was all, and the rest but a sigh? When did a struggling sentence structure last convey the loneliness of its author? Who, these days, shudders at the audacity of euphony? For whom was the bowing darkness of your homeless melodies meant?

Even if I could conjure up such beauty, all beat and bravery, I would not. Do you want them to topple you down? They loathe all oracular styles, as much as I loathe them. They loathe all that is style, as much as I loathe it. We think quite alike when it comes to matters of taste, me and this world that you wanted to pierce in the side. I cannot shelter you from the world: but I can keep you from reaching it.

Even worse still: if they were to appreciate it! Then this broken voice would no longer be mine alone.

She knew I too, like all members of our generation, dreamed of becoming a writer, and slowly I did become one. Not by exploiting her papers that I soon burned, but by *refraining from doing so.*

The misguided parodies that the mother performed have left an eternal residue of clumsiness in the daughter. Frieda always laughs too loud; she smiles too widely. Her large hands make extravagant gestures as she speaks of all the TV-stars she is acquainted with; how popular her sorry blog is, or all the musicians that line up to enkindle the exotic plant she smokes.

I guess she still has the same fits of sorrow, but she does not display them to me any longer. It is all my own fault: back then, I did not *earn* her trust – now I can partake in nothing but her glory.

Her eyes glow greedily when someone tells her of his success, later on she phones him and asks for money. Only rarely does she accept what her by now widowed mother offers her. Perhaps she cannot forgive the vicious arch of her mother's spine as it bent before her.

I still admire her: I still do. Those whitened scars that make her ripe skin reptile-like! Never did I see more avid generosity in a soul, never did purity haunt a being the way it haunts her: she cannot settle with less, with less than what is holy. All her whimsical tastes testify to it: she speaks of her tamed celebrities just in the same way as she dances, in a conscientiously sustained trance. She is blind to their imperfection, just as she is thankful for what little sublimity the drug can offer.

"You must try it," she insists. "You'll learn to become a better writer," she coaxes.

"I don't want to become better," I say, because no matter how hard I would try, I could never eclipse her.

I am jealous of my high and hungry cousin, who with diluted pupils swallows the saliva that now and again rises to her mouth.

I am jealous of the giddiness with which she invokes her losses.

I am jealous of her lifelong lack of recognition.

She is thirty-six years old now, wrinkled yet impossibly immature. She sits facing me, at a table by the window in the restaurant of her choice. She wears a dress with long green sleeves, possibly silk, certainly stolen from a friend, maybe even from a famous one. As usual, I am too cowardly to ask about the fabric; she would grip me by the wrist and have me touch it.

Like always when she knows that her cavalier will pay, she entertains. She entertains wonderfully well! Were I not held back by my role, I would have asked for an instrument or clapped my hands. Playfully, I would have slipped in a few bills between the straps of her sandals. I would have asked the waiter to dim the lights. Basked in darkness, she would have reminded me of her thirteen year old self. Her present and her past would have been painfully alike, and perhaps, then, I would have wept.

THE END OF SPECIES

Unlike other young men, Adrian did not for hours write forum posts lamenting the decay of an age in which even the lexical definition of "literally" has come to include "figuratively"; nor did he, like women his age, languish away for hours at the most far-fetched Slash[i] they can find on the web. He used the internet wisely. Without reflecting upon it, he had come to realize that a parallel dimension of nonsense had unfolded in our midst, and that this ever-present temptation stood in the way of what, at other times, might have been known as *purity of heart*. The insight that the unheard rumour of the most glorious heroes has been replaced by the deafening noise of virtual feeds, where a trifling, minuscule accomplishment always seeks its due recognition, would have brought a less robust nature to its knees.... He knew that there was a host of fanatical defenders of the internet, and of means of distraction in general, who claimed that it did not in any way preclude the seemingly unnatural profusion of artists in bygone eras, truly groundbreaking scientific discoveries or spiritual concentration skills, and even though he doubted them, simply because of the tone they used, so reminiscent of addicts claiming the compatibility of their drug of preference with whatever norms society sets, none of these possible losses were the actual reason why he, at an early stage, had decided to make but precursory trips in the virtual landscape. Nor was he, to tell the truth, as bothered by the infringements on his privacy as he claimed, because he did not see why privacy should be a right at all.... At least, he would rather enjoy the right of living in a commonwealth from which one did not wish to withdraw.

But it was ten years since he had stopped dreaming of claiming this right: ten years of sober decay.

Nonetheless, he *was* concerned that social media, the arena where he was denuded of all his human dignity, and reduced to a bundle of quasi-enviable qualities (his looks; his career peaks; his holidays and so on), should *also* be the archive which the intelligence of the enemy perused. If, at least, he could have been existentially humiliated and espied on two *different* sites, then he might have considered availing himself of social networks. His reservation stemmed only from his concern for purity; and whoever claims that purity goes hand in hand with searching for and reading through how rivals comment on photos of your ex, lies.

Now, his abstention and his competence (and, in his case, they were *one,* regardless of how much this pained the militant self-promotion promoters in his circles) had resulted in him leading a comfortable life, far from the maddening cloud of hypes in which his friends were engulfed. He had reached the status where he was at liberty to state, even at career conferences, that he was proud of belonging to the "entitlement generation", although he did not live up to its standards. Either, he said, the human species will soon be extinct, having by far overreached its productivity goals, or else we will have to be content with less quantifiable progress, abandoning infinite growth, forever. The so-called "entitlement monsters" of his generation were the only ones who realistically prepared themselves for the latter option; they alone could survive in a world where all one will do is to write poetry as robots feed one with grapes. For the former possibility, one cannot prepare oneself – unless by killing randomly for a bottle of mineral water. When he said so, the others laughed.

"At least become part of our network," they then suggested. "We promote young professionals, like yourself."

He was, what some virgins with taxonomic fury might well have labelled a top-SMV[ii] male in the making. Others would simply have called him "successful", and he was, by modern standards, both at the workplace and in bed. He loved, albeit superficially, women, but preferred being fellated by men, who were better at contriving the sensation of a vacuum he appreciated.

*

He rented an apartment in uptown Brussels, a light triplex. His bedroom was on the middle floor, together with the kitchen; the top floor was inhabited by Michel, a blond, bearded man with coffee-stained teeth, only slightly below average height, although he seemed shorter than that. Michel had a degree in sustainable development, but had changed course and was now an underpaid guide. He himself composed the routes and they were quite popular, perhaps since he had excluded all elements of "walking in the footsteps of the poet-child on the eve he shot his lover" from the tour. He was gloomy, because, as he confided to Adrian, after almost a couple of centuries of free trade, mass destruction was imminent: ten thousand species became extinct each year, and two thirds of the vertebrate animal mass on earth consisted of domestic animals that man, for no justifiable need, bred for food: almost two thirds of the (vertebrate) animal population are now lumps of meat swelling with hormones in factories. There was a zoological motif on his mousemat, and a plastic dolphin dangling from a thread attached to his desk lamp, while at the same time, he said, dolphins were either committing suicide in pools by crashing their sculls against the walls or suffocating in pollution at sea. How come the all but proven theory of evolution had not rendered human beings more humble, Michel asked himself. How come they still believed that they were the crown of creation, at liberty to condemn all other species to extinction?

Like most other lobbyists in their early thirties, Adrian too knew that some habits were inexcusable: working for a coal-mining corporation, or as a matter of fact almost any profit-driven company that meddles with politics; purchasing an unnecessary electronic device, more than one clothing item *per annum* or food wrapped in plastic; taking the plane – he knew that, in principle, one ought to be whipped for transgressions of such proportions. He knew that what was needed for the survival of all inhuman species was austerity on his part – and yet, by a quirk he shared with his coevals, he awaited new legislation that could check his greed; he did not abstain from anything, nor did he strive after bringing about the much-needed change himself. He loathed Michel's environmentalist friends, although he used their jargon for his jokes: how dared they impose *necessity* as a general rule to be followed…? (Albeit German, he had a very poor, almost English understanding of modality, and conceived of *the necessary* as an obstacle to be overcome in a bittersweet victory, quite like the first time he had raped a girl on campus.) And *one has to live* (or so he thought) even if living is earned by persuading drunken parliamentarians to conceal that one's employers sprinkle arsenic into the groundwater. He took the car to work everyday (even though that took him longer than walking), had a bloody steak every night, and, once a week, bought, preferably "exotic", prostitutes.

"There are no options to living like this," he said, and Michel despondently agreed.

"Indeed," he said, "for anyone who has ever even *come close* (within a fifty metre radius) to the European Parliament, there are none. Brussels is a city of lobbyists (the politicians may fall into this category), butcherers and paedophiles: there are no other professions here, and they all support each others' businesses."

"You're being very unfair," Adrian said.

"You're the one who brought it up," Michel said.

That was their first argument.

Later on, when they had forgotten it, they again discussed the destruction climate change was to bring about. Michel tabulated the statements he held for true:
1) Change in climate policies will have to be top-bottom; it will have to come in the form of bans and taxes;
2) This would not be possible without the abolition of fiscal paradises;
3) What private persons and grass-root organizations could do amounted solely to prolonging the timespan available for reforms on a greater scale;
4) However, they could not influence the general public, whose lethargy in these matters was well-known;
5) Hence, in order for substantial interim sacrifices to be made, those who acknowledged anthropogenic climate change would have to make atonement for those who did not; their sacrifices must compensate for the excesses of all the others.

"Surely you count me among those who can't be convinced?" Adrian interrupted him.

"Of course."

"So you make amends for me, as well?"

"Everyday I abstain from something for you; sacrifice is the driest form of prayer, and the only one I know."

"You make me feel like I'm already in purgatory," said Adrian.

And little did Michel suppose that indeed he was.

*

For night after night, Adrian had the strangest of dreams. By this incomparable suffering he thought that he made good for all his sins; this nocturnal insanity was the regular justification of his wanton meanness. But as of late he had begun to decode the message of these dreams. When he took time to decipher them *most premonitions proved right*. By following their guidance, he managed to get promoted;

to seduce his supervisor, and to survive a terrorist attack on a train.

He realized, of course, that he on his own could claim no universal validity for this voice, unless he convinced at least a hundred; not that anything would have been proven by the acclamation of the hundred. Certainly, he would still doubt it, as would anyone else. The issue was that, if he gained the people's support, there would at least be a faint possibility that what he was giving voice to converged, in the end, with the will of the universe. Like Rousseau's general will, his dreams could only be falsified; the belief of others could never verify them, only render their relevance slightly more probable....

To gain the acclamation of at least a few, he paid for an ad in the local magazine that was distributed twice every month, and wrote, in the laconic style called for by the genre:

"Voyant médium oracle pur au don héréditaire. Res ts vos problèmes: retour de l'être aimé, revolution, etc. Rep. internat. Il réussit où les autres ont échoués. Pai apr résultat confirmé. 0489018113."[1]

Some weeks elapsed without any client calling, and he began to suppose that his dreams were idiosyncratic; although they had helped him, on multiple occasions, their guardian god was too enmeshed in his personal business to bother about others.

Then, at a meeting, his cellphone vibrated; he instantly knew it was someone who wanted to exploit his inner oracle. So he excused himself and hurried to the WC (since

---

[1] "Seer medium oracle with hereditary gift. Solves all your problems: return of the loved one, revolution, etc. International reputation. He succeeds where others have failed. Payment after confirmed result."

he did not wish to be seen talking on the phone in the corridor), and as he was dialing the number, it called again. He picked up.

"Adrian Amsel," he said, "occult consultant."

"Monsieur Amsel?"

"Yeah, that's me." He observed the scribble on the walls. There was something heartbreaking about excavations finding out the same phalluses, the same vulvas, the same first pronoun in different tongues, the same superficial suffering on the same poorly drawn faces, transposed at so many insignificant sites, from immemorial times up till the present. These pen strokes were frail monuments raised to the unbearable pettiness of the human spirit.

"I know I should probably not contact you," the stranger said.

"Why not?" he asked.

"Because, unless your shield is sufficiently powerful, black magic always comes back at you."

"Everything always comes back at you: curses no more than blessings." He struggled to sound like a professional charlatan.

"But you're a black magician?"

"No," he admitted. "I'm no magician. I'm only someone who happens to know that there are traces of creation everywhere, and that these can be used for fortune-telling. As for me, I spot them in my dreams."

"My daughter has run away."

"Oh!"

"Is she safe?"

"Yes."

"What is she doing now?"

"She is… selling herself to someone quite rich."

"Is the sex good?"

"Not particularly."

"Will I ever see her again?"

"I can bring her to you. But I'll need some time…"

"Will a month or so be enough? Then I'll have to contact the authorities."

"How old is she?"

"Fifteen."

"Why did you not contact them already?"

"I'm afraid I might lose custody this time."

"Alright," he said. "But if ... I mean when I succeed in bringing her to you, you must pay me 5000 Euro by the end of the month, or I'll have to curse you."

"Can I pay by installments...?"

"Out of the question. Oh, and what is her name?"

"Joy."

Of course Adrian was glad he could be of some help. He reasoned, unbeknownst to himself quite like the ancient poet, supposing that if heaven had given him this talent, then heaven could not possibly let it go to waste. But as he returned home, long after midnight, and exhausted sank down into his bed, he felt exasperated. How was he to find something so rare as Joy in this impenetrable darkness?

*

"What are your plans for this weekend?" Adrian asked Michel the following day.

"My mother is coming this Saturday; we're visiting *the blue forest*."

"Can I come along?"

"Of course, although you should know she can't walk for very long."

"Even better: that shade of blue is best enjoyed *slowly*."

The name of his mother was Carmenta.

Michel welcomed her as Adrian was having his breakfast.

"How is José?" he heard him ask.

"He's fine."

"Who is José?" Adrian asked, because it *could* not be her man.

"My dog," she said, and when no-one commented, added, "When you have a dog, there is no need for religion."

After having stowed away her things in the guest-room, they headed for the forest, where the scilla still flourished. They parked the car at the lot. Adrian rushed to take out her wheelchair from the boot; she herself walked to it, as freely as if she had no physical defects at all. Adrian was astonished at this; he thought that the chronically ill were incapable of such feats. Then they slowly walked away along the asphalted path that followed the eutrophicated lake.

"Look, a swan," someone said.

Above them, the beech foliages were stirred by the wind, a sound that reminded Adrian of the sighs of admiring masses.... The rough trunk of the maple; the smooth and ashen trunk of the beech: both were aligned in the same inexpressible arborescent mission – and what was that? Adrian was unaccustomed to thinking; he strove almost violently after creating that emptiness is one's consciousness that is prerequisite for insights, and in the end he thought he had something that came close to an answer: *to be a tree is to be insusceptible to mutilation.* Each part of a tree is another tree. He imagined what it would be like to be human in this way: instead of having a certain personality as the outcome of one's traits, its – as it were – root components, one would have a thousand homunculi grafted on one's "person"; each moment would constitute an existentially separate individual, irreducible to the so-called personality.

He then perceived a small track leading uphill, and he realized that they had to follow it, since the female deer – the roes – had prepared it for them.

"Let's go *there*!" he exclaimed, and in an instant snatched Carmenta from her wheelchair, which Michel readily hoisted on his shoulder. She did not even laugh.

The sun was filtered through the foliages: a lace of light fell on them, and on the ground, where it enflamed the juniper needles, which were brown as wine in the shadow, and red as burning coal in the sun. The sprouts of young trees were growing there; the trunks of the more aged ones were coated in creepers. He did not tell her to be still, nor to hold fast; he did not dare ask her for anything. In carrying her, he was as patient and exclusively self-reliant as if he were ravishing her.

Their track slowly transformed into a ditch; although their burdens were light, they sunk to their ankles in fallen leaves, they nearly tripped over decayed fallen trees. The slope got steeper; they had to pass through a corridor of bowing birches.

"Oh!" screamed Carementa, because a cobweb had grazed her cheek: it was the kind of thick web that some spiders spin; it was like carded wool. They saw a beech with two trunks but with only one unique root system, and many other symbols of love, before they at last reached a grove scattered with scilla. Such a warm blue glow! It was as if the forest had been bruised at this soft spot.

In the light, they saw that the air was overloaded with the downy crystals of winged seeds. The air was pollinated with whimsical life; their pupils absorbed the painfully blue, almost purple note of the flowers; their hearts were full of gratitude; it was spring. Adrian could not stand it for long.

"Proceed!" he suggested. They climbed even further uphill. The conifers were slowly replacing the leafy trees; he felt relieved at this replacement. He finally put Carmenta down on a gigantic tree that the wind had uprooted and thrown over. Michel opened a bottle of the cheapest champagne he had found and not until she had emptied it did Carmenta notice that Adrian had filled the chest pocket of his creased holiday-shirt with leaves: a breastplate of inhuman veins. She also noticed the way Michel served him, as if he was aspiring to get him drunk.

"What is love?" Adrian suddenly asked.

"To no longer fear death," she explained.

"Do you fear death?"

"No."

"So you love?"

She seemed to deem a response at this point uncalled-for. The warm wind caressed their faces. Only in sun-plagued landscapes did Adrian appreciate this feeling of life. He saw a pale, almost transparent, segment of the moon linger in the sky.

*

"Minerva could not be wise, beautiful *and* sensual: that would ruin her divinity, and render her as unnerving as the God of the Old Testament, with his panoply of countless self-defeating traits. Since she is *both* the most beautiful *and* the best strategist among the goddesses she *must* also be cold. Likewise Aphrodite could not *also* be warring, and Mars could not *also* be wise. Just as the superiority of ancient gods consists in the tasteful sparsity of their qualities, so your mother is superior to us: she is all love, all paralysis, all deceitful silence," Adrian said when Carmenta had left.

"I thought you'd be bored," said Michel, somewhat ashamed.

"I was! And yet ... such exquisite boredom."

"That pretty much sums up my childhood."

"Who cares? I'm living it *now*."

*

The climate summit was upcoming. Adrian knew only because he saw how Michel's nails grew shorter and shorter, although the white crescent was constantly regrowing at their roots. The naked fingertips were as soft as those of the troubadour who sent his nails to his beloved. Legend has it these useless claws were presented to her on a pillow. His fingertips called those of a newborn's to mind, so harmless as to be almost threatening. For some reason Adrian did not wish to know how he so thoroughly had lost them. Perhaps their infernal softness put a check on his curiosity. In addition, the hollows beneath Michel's eyes assumed a warm, almost purple, shade of blue.

"You're hoping something will change this time," said Adrian.

"I am! But I know it won't."

"Why not?"

"Because only if the developed countries could pay for the developing countries' transition would this be even remotely possible. And of course they couldn't rely on private initiatives, but the funding would have to be public, stable and managed by an international organ such as the U.N. Also, the Intellectual Property Rights in sustainable technology must be, at least temporarily, suspended, to allow for the quick and unimpeded spread of the ideas on which the destiny of the planet depends."

This solution, albeit vaguely sketched, did not seem inherently unimplementable.

"So why couldn't they do this? Of course, the richer countries should pay more; anything else would be ludicrous. They'll only have to agree to a glorious loss."

"No ... they want to keep profiting from the transition. Or else they won't make it!"

"So we'll die out."

"Sooner or later."

"Does that bother you?"

"We'll take down all the other species with us as we fall; it bothers me that we'll be living, for a while, when they're all gone."

Michel's desperation was so great that Adrian did not meddle with it. In the end, Michel could not abstain from hitchhiking to Paris, dressed as a lemur. He knew it would not make a difference, but somehow thought that a lemur-delegate should witness the death-sentence that men and women, by sheer greed, were to pass on all life on earth. Only as he was packing his bag did he realize that he had promised to take his mother to the opera that weekend.

"Will you be my replacement?" he asked Adrian.

Since Adrian had never been able to deny lemurs anything, he let himself be talked into it.

*

It was June. The air was tepid, even the wind was warm; when the children at the edges of their groups hopefully turned about to see whether the howling of those at the centre had disturbed the passers-by, Adrian found them adorable.

On the street that lead to the opera, deaf mutes sat scattered on the benches, engaged in vivid conversations; over them, the pigeons came and went. One of them had wings marbled in brown, and a neck in mauve, as if its throat had already been cut. Above the lateral doors of the whitewashed theatre building, there were golden shields depicting Archangel Michael's slaughter of the dragon; and finally Melpomene and one of her sisters did their duty as caryatids. He then looked no more on the façade. Upon ascending the four steps to the main entrance, however, he noticed the shrivelling plinths, from which fell ice-blue flakes – the structure beneath seemed to be of a warmer hue, and almost like living flesh....

In the entrance, he found her. She had come directly from the railway station. He shouldered her bag and disposed of it in the wardrobe. He did not feel like explaining why Michel had not come: he preferred never to mention the rising fever of the earth. They took the elevator to one of the balconies. Of course Michel had bought her seats from which the scene could not even be spotted! The chandelier hung from the ceiling like a giant cluster of crystals; Adrian smiled at the profligacy of the passions of old people. The musicians tuning their instruments annoyed him: could they not have done this earlier? One hundred years later, they finally began to play....

The cowardice within him cringed before the music; it knew it would be extinguished, but it did not know its death would last only as long as the music. Time, to him, had always been the element in which he existed; a womb that at once inhibited and made possible his growth. But with the onslaught of *music*, time had suddenly unfolded in space: it had taken on all its dimensions: dolorous heights, vertiginous falls in pitch, and, through the spiralling movement of infinitely folded scales, even depth; it had rooms, arches, vaults and valleys: but to appreciate each successive construction he had to suffer. In the vehicle of music, time had become a palace of pain.

It would have been inexact to state that his contemptible person began to lose edge in the haze of sonority – because the music was more severe, more sharp, more crystalline, and *he* had been the haze, the stain on the lens of space that was now invaded by clarity. He had had no contours, he had been weak, but now he assumed the outlines of this alien strength; he became the lines, the curves and the planes of this translucent structure, erected without as well as within him, without heeding in the slightest the boundaries of his body. The music cut through him as if it were of a superior density, and he – this yielding matter, this pillar of sand, was altogether pierced by its divinely transient hardness.

He did not think, "I've lived without music – so I must die to it," because the mathematical composition of tones cared little for such pathetic sacrifices; although it evoked in him the greatest vulnerability he had ever known, it came from, and resurged into, a source beyond organic values. How little did it matter whether he lived or died, if this high C could be sustained a fraction of a second longer – the shrill victory of the coldest consolation; the metallic altitudes of the shortest vocal cords; the resonance of the widest chest and the most empty heart; an angelic incision in quivering flesh....

When the deafening applause and "Bravos" pronounced with the choked 'r' of the francophones, too far back in the palate for him to imitate, Carmenta profitted from the pause to tell him that this man has been endocrinologically castrated: that is to say that his voice was as unbroken as his body. At the very end, as they prepared to leave, he returned on stage, and sang "Lascia ch'io pianga".

Heavily thumped Adrian's heart in his throat at the first soaring imperative. "No!" he thought, as the soprano pleaded forgiveness. And like all lovers of beauty, he pledged an insincere oath: never to forgive, never to forget, never to deny this rare atomic glory: a glory more essential, more indivisible than any individual: a truth more indestructible than the heart of audience and singer alike. He clasped his soul's fist tightly around this nectar: the music, the lightning of this voice. He had always thought that eternity should be universally compressed in *any* moment, in order for there never to be a time in which it is not, and not like time, continuously spread over unfolding moments: but here eternity was impossibly contained in a few minutes, in just so many minutes as it took for him to promise that he would never forget it, and then forget it. He knew it had been beautiful, but forgot it had also been eternal; he forgot he had felt this beauty to be the prize of his entire life, the victory of his numbing spirit, the payment for all his humiliation, and so shall all likenesses of eternity be gone, one after the other, in this strange succession of broken promises that we call a human life....

*

"That was great, was it not?" Adrian asked, and Carmenta looked sideways at him. He had almost all the trappings of masculine beauty, especially when perched on the red velvet of theatre chairs, with his long legs crossed: she found him a sleek and slender giant, impeccably dressed; an ironically loud titan, who bothered everyone with his comment.

"This is all I have to live for," she answered. "So unlike you I can hardly call it *great*."

As they descended the stairs, sipping a drink in a plastic glass that they had been offered for free, to celebrate some anniversary of which they were ignorant, he looked at her for the first time: her hair was like a helmet of patina. The crooked fingers on her bony hands had nails painted in a silver green that reminded of the foliage of laurels.

He was certain she had *never* been beautiful, and therefore there was nothing pathetic to her present situation; she was no prima donna on whom admiration was taking its toll, nor an overthrown tyrant; she was not clutching at any bygone authority. She had had an insignificant life, it was now drained by an insignificant weakness; there was neither regret nor nostalgia in her pleasure in music. She would not let the poverty of her condition impoverish, in its turn, the pure euphony that had welled up within this concert hall, like a liquid structure superimposed on the space defined by the walls; a living structure as true to the human spirit as it was indifferent to it. She had valiantly endured so much beauty this night; he could barely bear the blissful pain of her expression.

That she had been ugly long before she became sick explained why she could sit enthroned in her wheelchair, gaze dimly at the bubbles rising in her glass and declare that she had nothing to live for but euphony and heart-rendering dissonance, *without* appealing to pity. On the contrary: she was enviable.

As he enjoyed the piercing sensation of envy – because his character was not *so* lowly and cheap that he did not appreciate being eclipsed by others, he heard someone repeat the name "Joy". He instinctively reacted to it, although at first he could not recall why. Then he turned around and saw the sweetest girl, who looked like she had escaped from the overly nostalgic lore of a humiliated nation, presently dragged away by the wrist. He hurried to follow the girl and the man dragging her. They mounted the grand staircase and turned left in the circular corridor outside the galleries; it seemed as if they had forgotten something at their seats.

As the man went back in, she waited outside, manifestly miserable. Adrian made some signs at her, but she only sullenly turned away. Not until he wrote the letters of her name in the air did she agree to talk to him.

"I'll go and get our jackets," she said.

"Wait by the wardrobe, I'll be there," ordered the man, who was crawling about on all fours on the purple carpet, presumably looking for his wallet.

Now it was Adrian who took her by the elbow and escorted her. Rather than descending the stairway, where they might be intercepted by the man, he made her follow him, until they found a row of seats in the dark from which they could not be spotted.

"Who are you?"

"I'm a medium; your parents have hired me to find you," he whispered.

"Please." She rolled her eyes.

"How did you meet?" he asked, looking in the direction of her companion.

"I saw an ad in our local newspaper; it stated that pretty students could earn well over two thousand Euro, net, for chatting on the webcam. I thought it was great deal, because I needed money."

"Why?"

"I try to give that amount monthly, to an organization that plants trees. You know about deforestation, I suppose?"

"Yes," he lied, and came to think of Michel. "I have a friend like you, he also loves life, and thinks it deserves to live."

"No," she said, "I'm not in it for life."

"What are the stakes for you, then?"

"Only a few weeks ago, we had a workshop in school about climate change. The lecturer said that he could understand those who doubt it, because indeed – there's uncertainty inherent in the models, aleatoric uncertainty as well as epistemic, and what we can have at best is always an approximation. What fascinated me was how we're computationally taming a chaotic system…"

"Hm?"

"Since the study object of climatologists is the *planet*, it's very hard to make clinical experiments. The experiments are, instead, conducted on simulations that are so complex that only the most advanced supercomputers in the world can run them!"

"So what's your point?" Adrian felt embarrassed at lacking even the basic high school level of science that evidently was critical for the seduction of this girl.

"Well, in a world where we wouldn't have made such technological progress, we wouldn't have known the damage we would then not have caused. But now that we do have the data I find it insanity not to let ourselves be redeemed by science. We've never before, collectively, as a species, acted upon scientific impulses alone: if we can only make it this one time, we will at long last become *homo sapiens*! And a new evolutionary era will begin!"

"But conversation on webcam wasn't sufficient?" he surmised.

"No ... Well, actually," she began, but then changed her mind, "It's complicated, you see."

"Come with me," he said.

"Never."

"I'll give you 2000 tonight; if you tell me the address of your school I can come there with the same amount tomorrow. But you should know, though, at your age, that there are some things that even a thousand trees can't make good."

"Perhaps, but not too many," she commented.

It so happened that he had just about four hundred in his wallet. They barely managed to get their jackets from the wardrobe when the rival perceived them; he called her name as they escaped through the gates and took off into the rain. They had to walk about for almost two hours before they found a functional ATM-machine, ready to offer them fifteen hundred. She put the rain-soaked bills in her shallow pockets but refused to tell him which school she went to. Perhaps she was not as dumb as he had thought.

When he returned, Carmenta was sitting beneath the triangular tympanum, behind columns of desirable uprightness. The theatre had already closed, and she had no keys to their place, where she was to spend the night.

"I'm sorry," he said.

"Don't be."

"Why not?"

"I've spent all this time sorting out my reasons for loving music so much. And, as I believe, melody is the only … *bond* we have."

"What do you mean by 'we'? You mean *us*?" he asked. She blushed.

"I meant us all…"

"You mean you weren't lonely at all, although I left you here."

"No."

"And why not…?"

"Because of … dam dam dam-da-da dam dam.…"

She had a surprisingly infallible sense of pitch, as her nails, polished with the colour of laurel leaves, drummed the rhythm against the armrest.

But, in the opposite bar, he drank too much before agreeing to hail a taxi, and when helping her into the backseat he scraped her veiny leg. She smelled so good, like an old, sentimental alcoholic full of love, and all the way back she was jangling her bracelets like a nervous little girl. In his ears, there was a cosmic truthfulness to the sound; it reminded him of the harmony of the spheres.

*

"I want to go to bed," she said, after having emptied yet another bottle of wine in his company, and grown weary of his poor conversation.

"No!" he said. Wearing only his pants, bare-chested, he paced back and forth like a caged panther, looking for the corkscrew. Now and again, his gaze lingered on her, as she sat in her wheelchair at the short side of the long dinner table, and she felt as if she had a fever. In his desperation, he grasped the champagne bottle and opened it with his teeth; when he spat some pieces of dark glass along with a mouthful of blood down the sink, she was, naturally, appalled.

He wanted to insult her, although he knew that most women only found it pleasurable when he swore at them.

"A woman like you.... You shouldn't...."

But what did he mean by *a woman like her*...? He had forgotten all about the limp body with its wrinkled limbs that he was presently shouting at; he was trying to address directly the invisible stringed instrument of her soul, suspended in the air like the intertwined jets of a fountain. He knew that divine melodies always plucked at these strings; he feared that they could never snap; he feared and admired her indestructible sensibility. And wherein did he think she had wronged him...?

He lifted her up from her wheelchair and carried her to the saffron coloured divan.

"Please, Carmenta," he said, "I've never known beauty before." She did not answer him. He stared a long time at the bruises on her wrists that the tubes had left behind: almost brown in the periphery, warmly blue at the centre. "I've never known beauty before, but now that you've showed it to me ... I suspect that it may save me."

"It can't," she said.

"But I don't want to become the corpulent middle-aged commissioner who, wearing an expensive chalk-striped costume and even costlier sunglasses, stands by the girls' marathon, whips the air with his headphone-cable and hurls insults at the runners on his way from work.... Or the man who celebrates his birthday alone at the fancy restaurant where he is a so-called *habitué, knowing* that they will have reserved a room for him and some exotic dancers with bellies like mercury.... Who at night stands lurking behind his curtains, and emerges from his lair whenever some pretty girl with a dog on a leash passes by, accusing her of spreading an animal stench in the neighbourhood, even grabbing her by the arm, if it be dark enough.... I don't want my life to revolve around tax frauds and petty revenges on those who both irritate and arouse me.

"I don't want my life to be all flayed tiger skin, young flesh at ever higher prices; all bribes and gourmandise; I don't want to be that brain-dead connoisseur, that mean expert, that cholesterol-laden heart which *infinite loneliness* no longer infuriates...."

And then, *she* touched *him*! She patted him awkwardly on the neck, as if he were a schoolboy defeated in a game of soccer.

"I don't want to become a swine – but I hold no grudges against swines, *they* aren't swines; unless already dead ones, stuffed with money: I don't want to become one," he went on.

"There, there; you're one already."

He suddenly knew what he wanted. He wanted to look after the dying, to defend the right of the dying to coloratura, to ever more intricate arias. He wanted to tell her this, but only succeeded in awkwardly seducing her; and his wish to gratify the dying was consummated there, on the sofa. Although she was so small she seemed by no means crushed by his weight. He grabbed her, as he thought, by her hair, and when the wig came off, he ejaculated.

"I've got to go to the toilet," she afterwards said, and he released her, upon which each went to their separate beds; both equally exhausted, one out of regained confidence, the other out of compassion.

*

The next morning, he had to tie her to a kitchen chair before he could even begin to fulfill her wishes. It did not take long. Then he rose from his knees, and drying his mouth he asked, with unforeseen coldness, "What else do you want?" But she only wept in response. When he saw her like that, he realized he had to be brought back down to earth before he could untie her; so he retreated into the bathroom. Upon seeing his own reflexion in the vast wall mirror, he found the warm golden glow of his skin almost blinding. "I do look like half a god," he thought, "or like three quarters a god, but that's hardly an excuse."

Then he heard steps in the stairwell; he heard how Michel inserted the key in the lock; he heard what a superhuman effort it cost him to turn it around, and for a moment almost fathomed the profundity of his friend's disappointment with his trip. He then blushed as he heard how Michel undid his knots; his mother's mortified sobs made his head spin. The thought crossed his mind that he should palisade the bathroom, fortify its door, and keep Michel from entering; but he knew that such ridiculous measures would only deepen his shame.

Of course, Michel came after him. He instinctively held up his arms for protection, but other than that patiently received Michel's blows, up to the point where the latter armed himself with a wooden clothes hanger. He then easily wrought the tool from his wronged friend and flung it on the floor.

"Forgive me," he said, without lowering his head or unclenching his fist.

He followed Michel who was heading to his bedroom, wishing he would be spared the most hysterical outburst of jealousy. He was not: Michel senselessly attempted to break his laptop over his knee, and then threw it on the ground and stomped on it; he then went on to tear down the paintings from the walls, shivering. Adrian knew that this pillage was not even directed at him, but rather gave voice to Michel's disappointment at the whole century.

"This costs you more than it hurts me," he said.

"Just leave," Michel responded.

*

Adrian had to lodge himself at a another friend's mezzanine. His friend would not come until late; he dined alone in a sushi restaurant in the neighbourhood. When at last his friend showed up and welcomed him, he was not impressed by this new accommodation. The apartment had a mouldy wall-to-wall carpet; the air was so moist he could hardly breathe. But there were books everywhere, especially catalogues of ancient astronomical instruments, and studies in cartography, which, next to the migration of mythological birds between ancient civilizations, interested this friend the most.

"The Sufi phoenix is, unlike its Chinese brother, a descendent of the filial phoenix that Hesiod observed," he said. "The phoenix is the most ascetic, sexless bird, the eremite among birds: unlike the swan, it deplores its resurrection and not its death.... In China it's a proverbial symbol of conjugal love: in the *Shijing*, for example – it's poem number 252, I believe – Huini unites the wings of male and female phoenixes as they fly together. But my favourite bird is the simurgh – it symbolizes how we tear ourselves asunder as we try to unveil God, because we are ourselves these folds in the veils, you know. Its Chinese counterpart is a *messenger of love*: the *qinghan*: you see the radical for speech in the latter pictograph. If we, as it were, fuse these symbols into one, then, the mirror in which you see yourself when you look at the beloved *is* the message; the reflexion against which you press your lips, without ever penetrating deeper, that is the message, the word in its entirety: do you understand?

But Rock, the symbol of rapture, as overpowering as Zeus, and like him, in favour of pretty prey, is in Chinese called *peng*, and symbolizes mostly scholarly success....

What can be gathered from these, and countless other examples, is that in China, sentimentality is as metaphysical as metaphysics was a matter of the heart for the Persians. There is a Persian saying, stating that no-one, dead or alive, has seen the Godhead – but one of his feathers – do you hear me? one of his feathers! – fell… and landed…"

"In China; you've told me this already. I'm tired," said Adrian.

"Of course," said his friend. "Make yourself at home. I'm sorry about the mould."

Although Adrian had the windows wide open in order to circulate the air, he woke up at 3:34 am, choking, and certain that he had received an oracle in his dream. He also surmised, somewhat dimly, that the dream had been caused by the discourse of his pseudo-ornithologist friend, but he knew that cause and meaning only rarely coalesce. The meaning of the dream was something entirely different from the question of which subconscious associations had brought it about; the meaning transcended even the strange workings of the brain. The meaning was like music! It relied on humans, but it was greater, or if it was not yet, it would be, one day.

He had dreamt that the soaring simurgh had dropped one of its feathers; he had taken it up; it was glass – immaculate glass that could not be stained by the blood of his hands. When he peered into it, there was nothing but light; the ray it reflected was like a snare; and hung in it, he saw humanity bathed, nay drowned in a soothing light.…

He reflected on his dream, but felt instinctively that he already knew what it was about: the quenched frenzy, which he had carried within for as long as he could remember, would neither abide nor unfold in his life, and eventually, it would kill him. It was as strong as a natural force, and thus equally strong as his strategic tameness; in their continuous mutual defeat of each other, these opposing inclinations created a kind of tension, and that was all he was. But, he now realized, the same thirst would break out afresh, in someone less polite, less pinionned: he would transmit his dissatisfaction to someone who was ready to suffer for change, someone less intent to spare himself and his reputation as a swine.

Since Adrian was not religious at all, he found that his hope was totally incommensurable with what eschatology taught, and in particular, its more naïve renderings, where eternity is represented as following upon time in a linear sequence; he was not into that idea at all. And nonetheless, *he who would come* would cure all disease, all greed that plagued their society, by revealing that they within themselves already had this power.

He expected his messianism to die down as soon as he rose from bed, but it did not. Throughout that day he was firmly convinced that humanity would soon enough be able to assume responsibility for its own destiny; he even dared mention his euphoria during the lunch break.

"We are law-givers," he said, "because we are the people, and we can found our own home. A home for all within city walls of music."

But his colleagues, who were each bent over their respective gadgets, only hummed in response. The internet had numbed their souls and moulded their desires in the same streamlined form; they wanted to decorate a bedroom, to bake some colourful cake, to go on a romantic holiday, to have their bile "liked" by others; in short, to extend beyond all measure their comfort zones. The niceties they collected online were planted like mines at the heart of what is most valuable in life: nature, love and longing after unity.... All of these were reduced to something nice: nice scenery, a nice dinner, a nice rape, complete with photographic evidence.

"Look, how cute," said one and showed him an advertisement, which presented a cartoon of a large-eyed white-collar worker seated at a desk, entitled "Effort time", followed by a soda, "Reward time".

"But that's horrible!" he exclaimed. "I'm not a pet I reward for the tricks I teach myself! I am a *human being,* acting out of duty or passion.... Or I want to act out of duty.... My foremost passion is my belief in duty," he corrected himself.

"Look, his identity has become incoherent ever since he deleted his network accounts!" Some mischievously laughed at him.

"You're wrong about 'duty'," another one interjected, "have a look at the article in this ever-available encyclopedia, will you."

"No, no! I will *not*! Can't we talk about it instead? Reflect on it together?"

"But there is no need for that; it's all written here!"

"Please," he said. "I beg you."

"Wait," they said. "We're busy."

When all are slaves, the only republican on earth crowns himself emperor, out of desperation. Perhaps *he who was coming* would have to resort to despotic means, for a while, because these people were so sedated on digital opiates that they could no longer be reached by words, or even by the sincere feeling behind these words, he thought.

As he, on his way home, emptied his purse and bestowed its contents on a beggar, he said, "I'm sorry, but soon there will be an end to all of this."

"Do you know what this is?" asked the beggar, as she exposed a bank-note to the sun.

"I know that it's coming to an end," said he.

"But do you know *what* it is?"

"No," he finally confessed.

"'Tis the devil," said the beggar and laughed.

"Oh!" he exclaimed. "I'm not religious," he then added.

"No: the religious don't believe in the devil," she said, and for some reason, he believed her.

He came home and found a cheque that Michel had kindly forwarded to his new address: his reward for having retrieved Joy. The demon slowly emerged from the envelope. "Satan!" he thought, "I swear it's him! The angels represent us – our capacity of adoration, of sincerity.

When, in the Koran, Satan alone does not kneel before Adam, this surely means that some faculty of ours deceives us, and will not obey us, although it is *ours*: and what is money, and the worth of money, but an expression of our most irrational and subterranean impulses…. We have taken the darkness from within and printed it on paper: that's money."

The liberator Adrian had dreamt of would rewrite the laws in accordance, not with what we had hitherto been, not in accordance with what is extinguished, but in heeding what is still smouldering in the ashes…. In abolishing money, the saviour would extirpate richness and poverty alike; what was to be founded by him would differ from ancient Lacedaemonia in that the Helots would be replaced by machines. Finally, we had reached the technological expertise that permitted all to live in freedom and frugality, and as soon as the as yet unborn stranger saw this, he would realize our hopes: he would prove beyond all doubt, for all to see, that freedom and frugality *are one*.

Although he would, in one sweeping movement – like the poet, who with his sleeves grazed all the mountain peaks – uproot all greed and slavery, he would not blame those who had succumbed to it, he would pardon them, and say, "Mammon was necessary; he was a worthy enemy, but the spear of our generosity is *so long* – it pierced him and nailed him to a distant star!"

There would be science and art: this new world would be driven by emulation, love and sacrifice – forces Adrian had never known.

The bank-notes Adrian paid with had always burned his fingers: now he knew that they were also chains. They were worthless sheets of paper! There was no natural reason for us to abide by their dictates: none. There was no equation between their entirely imaginary worth and *life;* moreover, there should be none. The starving did not crave for money; what was needed was justice, severely constitutionalized justice, and societal organs that supplied all with what they needed, if not more. Perhaps, at first, they could institute a currency of their own, and dictate its value, thus discrediting their credit rating; this was the first, indispensable step in the elevation of politics over economy. After that, they could slowly phase out this interim currency as well. They would then make one giant fire out of it, to celebrate that after a long and seemingly endless winter, the spring of freedom had come!

Now, Adrian would have worked, and a hundred times harder, for no monetary recompense at all, as long as he had the means to survive. He would have worked a thousand times harder if his salary was burnt: if he, by working, could earn the extinction of money, he would have shouldered the yoke and died as a beast of draught.

His dream had miraculously exiled him into that proverbial desert in which the true value of jewels and gold is revealed to the wanderer. In this desert, everything appeared more bright, more splendid. The nimbus of *thirst* surrounded all things. He knew he would not survive this thirst – but, as a species, they would, thanks to him who was coming, because surely he would come.

His euphoria was spreading, like a poison instilling itself in the tissue; he was becoming one with this strange immaterial body. He had never known such joy before; he felt like the tranquil vessel of an overpouring ecstasy. He sweated as he lay between his sheets, the high windows wide open; the sound of the gathering storm gave voice to his confused hopes.

*

But that night too, he was awakened by a sense of imminent disaster: again, he had had a dream. This oracle was not like the one that had preceded it. But how could he differentiate one premonition from another! It did not strike him that one might be true and the other false, and since he did not wish to give up on his budding faith in humankind, he accepted both. Sitting on his bed, with his chin leaning on his knee, he said, "I'm the one who has sown this seed.

I'll be the father of this godly creature: the Messiah will sprout from my stem." Then he procured a gazetteer from the bookshelf and at random put his finger on a district: Dinant. The home village of Michel, and Carmenta, too.

He had transmitted something she had received – and indeed, it was most fitting that humanity's new life should spring from so barren a source; he felt as if he had witnessed a budding plant sprouting from a corpse.

*

Nine months later, he rented a car.

He listened to the radio as he drove. The classical station was broadcasting two Rachmaninov operas live. In *Aleko*, pain had been cast in the mould of moonlight. A caravan of sorrow marched, on light feet, through his soul as he heard the theme, at once lulling and heartbreaking. He marked the time of the music by beating the steering wheel with his shaky fingers.

In *Francesca da Rimini*, the souls were but whirling wails, entangled in each other, and the bows of the cellos cut the diameter of these downward spiralling plaints, like the hollow wind that wrecks infernal lovers. Francesca implored Paolo to erect, instead, the celestial temple of love, but he refused, and, touched by the beauty of this refusal, she conceded to die forever. But even in death, she had to relive her betrayal of life. "Memory is hell," Adrian agreed. But unlike Francesca and Paolo, he could not recollect a kiss worthy of eternal damnation; there had been no ecstasy in his touch, because in gripping he had not lost grasp of the yonder side…. In eternity, if there is such a thing, he would only remember how the wig had come off, like a ripe fruit that yields to the hand, and that something, perhaps sadness, had prematurely climaxed at that point. The insatiable hunger of the souls the music portrayed was now *everywhere,* like a counterpoint of longing – and in that instant, he knew it had been there long before he had turned the car radio on, this hunger of the damned. Its stitches of wind were sown into all space he passed; he drove faster, but it hovered over the fields, in the clouds heavy with rain; he could not escape it.

After some hours of driving (in his agitation, the GPS had repeatedly deceived him), he arrived at the small house, surrounded by high hawthorn bushes. She was seated in the garden, under a blooming fruit tree; the flowers looked like a myriad of small bridal veils. He hastened to her side, knelt before her and exclaimed, "My son!"

"I aborted it," she said, listlessly. And as she saw his expression, she added, "Adrian, please, what's wrong with you? I'm well over fifty years old."

(ONE SHADE OF) STARVED FIRE

I

In this immaculate city, the heart of global trade in stolen electronic gadgets, he was her only lover. Here there was not a trace of the almost holy dilapidation we are so fond of worshipping in other habour cities, on the verge of inundation. The skyline crested with commercial pinnacles, the drowning sun and its polluted glow, triumphantly golden, evoked neither the rottenness of Venice nor the midday-timelessness of Bangkok. *This* city might not be immortal, she thought, but the blue of its lagoons surely is. The melancholy of the crowds – as sweeping, as transient as the ideal of one's youth – will prevail, even after the death of its individual elements….

After one night, she had turned him down. She had glimpsed the immensity of his heart; she would not have this immensity "like" all the semi-pornographic images of herself that she had published on some social network, which he was bound to do if they parted, if she accepted him as her "friend". Those would-be platforms are truly webs, where lovers are caught and devoured alive by the spider of totalitarian taste that ordains them to "like" coffee and sex; pool parties and promotions; pastry with idiotically pretty glazing; click-baiting fake news and catchy updates in the moment of death.

"I see," he said, and instead asked for her telephone number.

She denied that she had one. She had only a name, that was also a trademark. In addition, her name had in a recent coinage been transformed into the verb of refusing to wear socks with jeans: that said just about everything of how fashionable she was, and how little contact she had ever enjoyed with that waste of innocent blood otherwise known as *reality*.

They met for the second time in the expatriate club's monthly masquerade. The first thing he said upon recognizing her was, "You shouldn't always wear blue."

Had her aspiring lover really said that? Could they still be so trite, so presumptuous, so … She could not hold her alcohol. She had relished the liquefaction of character it had brought on. As a gentleman, he had let her puke into his hands to spare the sheets with her family monogram.

Then, to compensate himself for that courtesy, he read aloud from her notebook as she still lay in bed, unable to extort it from his grip:

"10 commandments for a 22nd century thinker …"

She listened, flushed, to the concatenation of prohibitions of which she was the author.

"'§7: Only pursue science when all other possible incomes have been exhausted.

"'§8: Then leave, for good.

"'§9: But where, but where?' …. A question is not really a commandment," he objected.

"My English isn't very good. I don't speak it very often," she explained.

"Ha! You don't improve your English by speaking it. On the contrary, that's how you ruin it."

"That sounds like my native language…"

He went on, "§10…"

"Please stop," she said, "it's too embarrassing. I'll do *anything*."

"I'd like to hire you," he said.

"No, I couldn't accept that. It resembles too much all other job offers I've received."

"You know, some scenes will keep on recurring until you … until you accept their recurrence."

Some scenes are the kernel around which a life is wrapped. In a previous incarnation, she had been a princess, and he a slave growing up at court, later to become a servant in a Zoroastrian temple. He could never forget her. When, by chance, years later, she travelled by in her sedan chair, she had found him sound asleep, and upon recognizing him, she had left her earring: when he woke up and saw it, he turned into fire and burned down the temple. Centuries later karmic sentimentality (缘: *yuàn*) had made them find each other again, even in an inhospitable expatriate community. In this life, he was an HR-manager and she a philosophy graduate who had run away, alone, with some undeserved prize-money. His name was Mengran, and hers was Beatrice.

As a tall, skinny and – above all – blonde girl in Asia, it was initially not difficult for her to track down modeling jobs. Most shoots involved long floating dresses. Her merchandise consisted in the alleged beauty of her race. A high and broken nose-bone, a well-rounded forehead, a scull worthy of the appreciation of Herman Lundborg. Piercing grey eyes and silken hair that came off in fistfuls. *They* did not shun her beauty. Perhaps it was rather their acceptance of it that had caused her first outbursts of anger. Since she became known to be difficult, she was recruited for fewer and fewer photo shoots. She also had to go abroad soon to renew her visa.

She was running out of money, and heaven knows how she would get on when all was gone. That was why he wanted to offer her a sinecure.

Of all absentees of the past few centuries, she was certainly the worst. She hated the country she lived in but returning home would be to admit defeat. Her disgust was not like that of the transitory guests who were her friends: theirs was a distaste homeward bound, certainly petty, but designed to amplify the virtues of their own civilization upon their return. Hers was a hatred of a different brand, bordering on the maniac. What had lashed her into this arrogance, no-one still knows. Her colonial fury was more akin to that of Vasco da Gama than to the obsequious envy of saint Matteo Ricci.

She told him that she was a Swede, and, as a consequence, blue-eyed, "We're so fearful of being called 'racist' that we've sold what little culture we had; we've sacrificed it on the altar of the politically correct." She further told him she would rather move to Iceland and live there, because of their stricter immigration regulations. Notwithstanding, she lived in this Chinese metropole, which was both pulsating and strangely at bay, immersed in an artificial bluish light. Meanwhile, she posted Youtube-comments in her real name, "I seriously think that all Asian people should be annihilated." Etc. She found herself *very* incorrect; it was a major turn-on that fuelled hours of self-conceited fantasy, *"I'm so cocky!"* she then thought, if indeed girls priding themselves on their "outspokenness" can be called *thinking*. Her self-appreciation ("cocky; smart; controversial; skinny; unchaste") mimicked that of millions of privileged young women her age and seemed much too reflexive to be the outcome of a genuine thought process.

She had crossed the ocean for *this,* for this hateful loneliness, driven by that strange amalgam of boredom and curiosity that spurs backpackers on. Like the host of backpackers that poured into town that year, she had come under the banner of fast internet connections and cheap coffee. Like them, she too was sinewy and liked to be photographed. Although they believed themselves to be travelling, they had never moved one foot in any direction; they were perpetually immobilized, frozen in their superiorly experienced poses. Most backpackers she knew had since then moved on, and travelled to the poorest, and hence most generous, regions in the world, to beg for food. She admired them, because at any point they could order their families to send them a yacht that would bring them home, and yet they preferred to wallow in dirt, and when possible suckle the breasts of starving girls who have no money to give. In return they would post a photograph of it on their travel-blog, under the heading: How to Live for Free in the Third World; she "liked" it, but disliked the imperfect teeth of the poor. The widely-begged backpackers she knew were like missionaries preaching the gospel of random rapacity and universal cluelessness; they had convinced her that she, too, was wise beyond her years, simply because she could afford long flights.

"Out of all virtues," she thought, "curiosity is the most lethal. Never have we been this curious nor has there ever been less left to discover on earth." Yet she had something left to discover. She had.

II

"You dropped the A-bomb on the Japanese and you surely don't hear them complaining," she said. "Because they're adults: this is a nation of babies."

"One of the bombardiers was a relative of a friend. Even if it were only for his suffering afterwards – it wouldn't have been worth it. The war had already ended," commented an American, soberly.

"The Chinese exaggerate everything. They believe Nanking" – she purposefully mispronounced it – "was on a par with the holocaust." Then she burst out laughing.

"Genocide aside," punned a young Korean. "My grandmother was a 'comfort girl' in a Japanese encampment…. And even the Japanese suffered irreparable losses. The Chinese weren't the only victims of the war."

"But you would think so!" said Beatrice in a tone that would have qualified as hysterical, had not that word fallen out of fashion. "You would think so judging from the way they talk: piles of chopped off heads; lamp-shades of human skin...." She laughed even louder. Then she raised her glass and yelled, "To lamp-shades!"

Like most expatriate communities where restless young adults come together, regardless of location, this too was inveterately racist, even if all of its members were not. Now they were assembled, and therefore they only smiled at her insanity, whereas, if they had been alone with her, they would have left, out of decency.

At that time, a clip was circulating on the internet. There was a white man, muscular – but not in a healthy sense – looking quite doped, to be honest, who, at night, on an open street, stood humping a young girl whom he held fast, as she sprawled before him. You could see her hips glisten in the darkness. She wept and repeated over and over again, in a haunting monotonous voice, "*Wo bu renshi ni, wo bu renshi ni*" (I don't know you, etc.). The man was encircled by other men, who kept at a safe distance from him, and advanced only now and then to strike him. Then there was a cut in the clip. In the next scene, the police had arrived on the spot. The presumed perpetrator lay grounded, bleeding from the head. Some civilians nonetheless profited from his helplessness and kicked him in the belly. Insults were hurled at the unconscious.

The expats were *in shock*. First, said a Belgian, how would this interfere with the image of foreigners in China? Chinese society might become even more closed, due to the sick suspicious atmosphere that this clip cultivated. Second, said a fellow Swede, it was obviously manipulated. The cries of the girl just did not seem quite convincing, in his experience.

The Chinese who were there all courteously agreed on the outrage of kicking an already defeated opponent. Among them was Mengran. He stood next to Beatrice.

"I'm not afraid of you because of this," he assured her.

"You're too close," she said. "You all smell the same."

They all agreed that the clip was arranged, by xenophobic computer geeks. The internet brims over with such vipers, but in the media she consumed only Chinese virtual haters were ever portrayed as actually representative of a funnily skewed public opinion. Surely, since the journalists put their trust in these testimonies rather than in statistics officially gathered and made public by such a deceitful nation, the expats agreed that the clip was poorly cut; anyone could spot the artificiality of it. Especially the girl, who deigned to show her buttocks in this shrewd piece of propaganda, compromised its scheme.

"An actress, and a bad one at that," an Englishman concluded.

The general denunciation of this supposedly theatrical rape struck a chord within Beatrice's soul. A desire to drown surged within her, and so she drank more. Mengran, ever composed, observed. When she was sufficiently unconscious, he followed her on her way to the smoke corner, and said, "I can see that you're sad. I don't know why you're like this, but you should know that everyone here can see it."

Exasperated she talked to a guard and insisted that Mengran should be expelled from the club, at least for tonight, but preferably forever. But she talked too incoherently to get her intention across.

Towards the end of the night, the two men she had spent most of the evening with were preparing to leave with her. Each had one arm around her waist.

"No," she protested. "I'd rather go with him."

Mengran lent her his arm without even looking at her. They hailed a taxi, as blue as a caricature of the sky.

"You're angry," she said with satisfaction.

"Women don't make me angry," he said, and the tone of his voice was proof of his sincerity in this matter. What hideous chivalry his manners bespoke! She hated him and his phlegmatic adoration.

"Women really aren't human in your eyes, are they?"

"Few people are human..." he commented, evasively, and even the taxi-driver laughed. A smug laugh masked as a cough.

She was infuriated but her nausea got the upper hand. They had to pull over and let her vomit on the sidewalk. He was immediately at her side, with a handkerchief. He seemed not a man, but an infinite paper supply.

"Where should I take you..." The falling pitch of the phrase made it sound rather like a musing than a question.

"Home," she said, between two bouts of sickness.

III

He carried her upstairs

"I don't like it when you're this kind," she whispered.

"Well, what *do* you like?"

"You're only interested in me because of my hair," she said without emotion, and added, "They call it *golden!*"

"It's true that I like gold," he confessed. "And so what? What would become of us if we didn't have faith in a hierarchy of metals?"

"But why gold? It has always been gold, long before we charted the elements according to their chemical properties."

"Because it glows without warmth. It's like starved fire."

"Couldn't we use fire instead of money, then?"

"Oh, I'd like that!"

He awkwardly patted the protrusion of the sheets that gave away her leg.

"But Beatrice ... " he relished her name. He pronounced it with such delicacy it no longer referred to her. "Be honest: what do you like? I'm groping in the dark here. Just tell me, and I'll change."

"How much?"

"Try me. I'm more malleable than you think. I used to be poor, you know; poorer than you've ever been."

"Well, for starters, your skin doesn't please me."

"You prefer fair skin? That's certainly a surprise." His irony was not acerbic at all. It was almost soothing, as if all cruelties she could think of were justified since they could not exceed the span of his expectations.

"You're wrong: I prefer either extreme paleness or total darkness. Your skin is neither, so I find it ugly."

"I'll bleach it," he said without hesitation.

"Rather get a tan," she said and regretted it, since in his mind this would add up to a compliment. A remorseful silence ensued. In a vain attempt to hide his gratitude, he laughed, and concluded, "Is that all?"

"No!" she protested, too eagerly, and then explained, slowly, as if she were talking to a child, "I *really* don't like it when you're this kind."

He lapsed into thought for a few seconds, before stating, with resolution, "Oh! I'll be mean." She knew he lied, and yet acted on this lie.

IV

"I'll carry you forever," he said, a few weeks later, in blissful ignorance of the curse he thereby incurred. He wanted to lay his head in her lap; he wanted for them to be as contemplative, as still, as lovers of yore: like Sima Xiangru and Wenjun, or like Zhang Chang and his wife with eyebrows as thick as caterpillars. But Beatrice shoved him off, because she was writing on a small, almost perfectly flat keyboard, by which she was required to curl up to the point where her breasts were almost perfectly flattened against her thighs: thus there was no room for his head in her lap.

"Leave me alone," she said.

"What are you doing?"

She showed him, in triumph, the fruit of her "labour": an impossibly public intimate journal... And – alas – all that he had bought for her, all that he had intended for her consumption, had, in eternalized form, wound up on her blog; item after item followed upon one another in a long parade that ridiculed his, admittedly too material, seduction. She even wrote how much it all had cost!

She had had her teeth whitened: they almost glowed in the dark, and she held up every item close to her inhumanly lucid smile. She also listed what she wore – which brands she preferred, and how many workers had burnt alive in their factories; she gladly supplied the opinion polls that showed that young fashion consumers, as a rule, do not take the ethical dimensions of production into consideration when they purchase their ugly and brittle merchandise – she adduced these investigations as a *ground* for not caring! Her blog was so poorly written his eyes hurt; half of the bad orthography and countless anacolutha were contrived, half were inborn: she wanted to come off as the idiot she was, because she knew that idiocy is the sole virtue of consumerism, and she wanted to impersonate this virtue.

Having allocated all her spiritual filth to the body, she documented her frequent purges, but of course these measures were of no avail: her idea of cleanliness was so confused, and her asceticism so compulsively selfish. Before taking a bite of her meal (always based on animal protein) and hastening to the toilet where she vomited it all up, she would have to photograph it. This digitalized metabolism was, of course, duly recorded online as well, as most of her other bodily functions. It was as if she thought that she could absorb nutrients through the lens. And maybe she could indeed survive thus, because as far as he could see, if she had accurately listed her intake of calories, she should have died of starvation long ago. And maybe, he poetically thought, she had.

And as most freely eating disordered *photographees* of her sex, she was against the male-dominated power structure in Western societies, although it was unclear how men impeded her food intake; on the contrary, men had always tried to feed her. She wrote about men on her blog, mostly flowery calls to chastise them for her own endurance in self-imposed starvation, for the lack of a sufficiently mellifluous, and yet not too condescending, euphemism for female masturbation, and, most of all, for not finding her hilarious when she reiterated this kind of self-righteous nonsense. In particular, she called out for all those men in power, whom women instinctively seduce but soon get bored of, to suffer for having exploited weaker creatures. The chastisement she preferred was, of course, castration. She was as fascinated by it, as the etymology of the verb "fascinate" can intimate.

In response to all this unexpected bile he asked, with genuine interest, "I thought you were almost perfectly emancipated in the West...? In which particular area do you not yet enjoy equality of opportunity?" Of course, she only swore at this. She loved to swear; she thought it was *empowering*.

As they grew closer Mengran became more and more inclined to see her as the symbol of the self-centeredness that threatens to ruin more than half of the body politic in richer countries – because what shall one make of political subjects who cannot differentiate between the concepts of "choice" and "justice"? Never has an era been more superstitious, and never have superstitions been so shallow. She wanted badly to belong to the choicest circle of "it-girls", who were like the *pharmaka* of ancient Greece. In reproducing, as if in a fervour, images of them, we ritually extracted them; publicity was our vapid version of human sacrifice. Which disease were they blamed for? Which contagion did they represent? Surely it must be the impossibly feminine hysterical howl at the name of luxurious brands, this parody of maenadic frenzy. And this was what Beatrice most craved; this was why she so often dressed in white blazers, had an expensive woven basket dangling from her arm, and would refuse to wear socks with jeans even if he pointed a gun at her heart.

He pitied her helplessly; she knew so little, much less than her stupidity could even begin to justify. She knew which materials were in vogue, and then of course, she knew all about how pain is converted to pleasure. Only in her opinion pleasure was but a sequence of pains, of the right intensity and well-ordered. That was how Nietzsche had defined it, at least. Pleasure is the pain of something gradually yielding, whether this be your girlfriend or your sanity. Pleasure was thus equally proportional to the strength of the resistance and the strength of the invading force, and that was probably the reason why people no longer knew pleasure, she thought. They were too weak for it.

If she had to choose between the accounts of Freud, Kraft-Ebbing and Schrenk-Notzing, all unmatched pioneers, she would choose *early* Freud, prior to 1920, revisionist footnotes notwithstanding. Your humble author reluctantly admits that this preference does indeed deserve a beating. But *Beatrice's* masochism certainly was not primary; it was an entirely narcissistic deviation of an original desire to harm. Whether other forms existed or not was of no interest to her. She did not care, as long as she got to mimic the pain she would have liked to inflict. In order for it to be that very pain and no other, she was dependent on well-trained expedients.

Naturally, she did not mention how poor novels had catalyzed her to deviate, if what is at least as common as the norm can indeed be called a deviance. This statistical fib was necessary to transform a previously universal phenomenon into the thrilling stuff of best-selling novels. Long gone were the days of the mystics, and although no-one would wish for them to return, it was sad that sensations of existential rapture were presently entrusted to a few bodily orifices, whereas before they had also overflowed the soul, into the vastness of the universe.

Inhaling just a little amyl nitrite would help her from collapsing; because her pain threshold was so low, and she had always fainted at the sight of blood.

Her explanation of her tastes was quite magisterial. Mengran seemed bored to death.

"I can't hit you. How could I? You can't talk me into what is impossible – *especially* not like this."

He refused to sign the unilateral, and surely aberrant, BDSM contract she had presented him with. In doing so, he thwarted her destiny, and all obstacles thrown in the path of destiny must be disposed of, somehow. Her destiny was *enslavement,* she explained. If the cost of this would be enslaving others, then so be it.

"If I by nature have this ... preference," she said, "then how could nature leave it unfulfilled? Its fulfillment is as inevitable as a law of nature – and *of course*, you can abstain. But then I don't want to see you again."

"天生我材必有用 (*tian sheng wo cai bi you yong*)," he said.

"What?"

"Nothing."

"And don't advise me to search for help. First of all, I'm too stupid for therapy to have any effect on me."

He did not really know what was meant by the word "therapy".

"I won't love you for long if you stay this way," he threatened, with a voice so soft it was barely human.

But she pathetically insisted, and in the end, she won. He bent her little head, so akin to an abandoned, ashen bird's nest, backwards, buried her face deep in the pillow and humiliated her with the remote control (making sure to first remove the batteries). Afterwards, his remorse procured him a vile migraine. But she claimed that this did not even come close to what she deemed satisfying.

Once, he awaited her with his son. Beatrice did not even know he had one.

"Show me a picture of the mother," she demanded.

Mengran signaled that he rather not speak of the mother in front of the child.

"He doesn't understand me anyway," said Beatrice contemptuously.

"My mother is very beautiful," commented the child.

Mengran sighed and showed her the family photo he kept in his wallet.

"Not especially," said Beatrice with ire.

"*I* think so," said the child.

"Why did you love her?" she asked Mengran.

"She summoned me, well all of us, to change our lives; to become more alive."

"Then why divorce?"

"Please," he responded. "Please, no more of this." And then, he miraculously yielded to her sordid provocations. He pinched her arm. Very carefully at first, but as he heard how her breathing became more superficial, he pinched harder, embedding the nails in her skin. Soon, he had passed the point of no return.

Afterwards, he would untie her, almost on the verge of crying.

"Do you remember the masquerade?" he said. Of course he knew that a friendship is over at the very moment when you decide on which memories to spare! Of course he knew that slipping out of oblivion also means leaving the realm of intimacy.... But he must have been desperate, he must have thought that there was nothing left to lose.

"Yes," she said, "I remember it all." How *dared* he destroy this moment?

"I thought that, for the first time in my life, my prayers had been answered."

"And now? What do you think now?"

But he could not prolong the conversation. He had to go on a trip to Singapore and he was already late for his flight. Nowadays, he gave her all his salary, without asking any questions. She purchased new instruments of torture with it. The games bored him and soon he would bear it no longer. She decided that, before he left her, she would repay his weakness.

V

She and four Scandinavian friends from the modelling agency made an excursion to the hot springs.

They made fun of the artificially flavoured springs, which were imaginative and florid, like ice cream tastes: wine; lemon; milk.... Of course Asians had to mock nature; they had no sense of measure. A word like *sophrosyne* surely had no Chinese counterpart – not that they were very knowledgeable about abstract nouns in Chinese, but they knew *enough* already.

Some tattooed men, who claimed they were Japanese, were flirting with them; her friends wanted to leave, but she stayed. She waited till her friends left the pool and then glared at the admirers, to intimidate them with her unapproachable air, to hurt them for trying to offer her gifts. It served them right. One of them looked very much like Mengran. It could have been his younger mafioso brother. She had never been able to exercise any control over her mind, which now rehearsed the dénouement that had taken place not long ago, soon upon her decision to punish him for having first stooped to obey her, and afterwards been meaning to leave her for so long.

After one of their sessions, she had limped to the police and reported him. The evidence of all physical harm she had freely suffered testified eloquently in court. Even though he could afford a good lawyer, he did not hire one. He had golden knees, as the saying goes; he was unbendable and thus bound to break. Perhaps by abstaining from defending himself he became an accomplice of the verdict; that way he had to blame her less. And she knew he would acquit her, to the extent that that was still possible.

After two weeks in prison, he hanged himself. A not insubstantial amount of his wealth he had bequeathed to her; he had made this change in his will early on in their relationship, and for some reason he had not changed it afterwards. Probably he had been too distracted by the charges.

That was how their story ended. Perhaps she had stayed in the pool not out of spite, but because she had first mistaken the stranger for his ghost. She was terrified at the thought of his spiritual remnants. She knew his ghost would haunt her as he had wooed her: patiently, from a distance, and with unwearied love.

Advance Responses to Sanja Särman,
Beyond Brightness

From Laura Kipnis,
Professor, Northwestern University, USA and author of *Against Love: a Polemic* and *Men: Notes from an Ongoing Investigation.*

Sanja Särman writes with extraordinary originality and wit – and more than a dash of gleeful perversity – about the inner landscapes and emotional transactions of cosmopolitan life. If you wish to map the fate of the Self – does it even still exist? – in these dislocated times, Särman has established, with *Beyond Brightness*, that she owns the question.

From Jens Klitgaard Nelsson,
Editor in chief, *Brevnoveller* (an editorial and literary movement for short fiction in Sweden).

I'm not an academic and I am a foreigner reading this book in my second language, a barrier that has been greater than I thought and I'm afraid that this has made my reading less colourful than it could have been if I had had a more direct access to my reading "register", to the nuances and the depth of thought, as well as to my professional, intellectual approach. So, I decided I had to take the title of the book literally, I had to go "beyond brightness" in order to give a response that could give this book and my reading of it, justice. And such reading had to be purely emotional, down to the core in me. I had to accept that things would be lost in translation – like the deeper sense of context and references presented to me – and rely on my own stripped understanding of the characters and the stories. Although this is in one way a lessening of the experience of the book, I also consider that my reading it more intuitively in this way could add an important dimension to the understanding of it, because what I think Särman really wants to say with this book lies not only beyond brightness. It lies beyond thought.

It didn't take me long to find a feeling of what I've just read in Särman's collection of destinies. And that is – that humanity is what's complicated, not science, not nature, not music. That the world and the people who inhabit it, no matter if they are from Hong Kong, Stockholm or Brussels, are terribly alone in this society and the expectations it imposes on us. The strength in Särman's short fiction lies in embodying her somewhat twisted characters, their thoughts and actions, when they reach an emotional state of inevitability.

What better example of this than the scene where Adrian is in the opera together with Carmenta, his friend's handicapped mother? Adrian first approaches the spectacle with a layer of scepticism, but then, seconds later, when experiencing the beautiful vocal tones of a castrato singer, feels eternal clarity trapped in the length of the sounding music. Oneness has struck him. Later, nothing will ever be the same, hence his tragedy is in knowing too much, too late.

This is not a collection of stories about people who escape their destinies, it is about people who see it coming, partake in their given roles out of necessity and, sometimes almost delighted, play them up to the end. That, I believe, is the true nature of the modern tragedy of which Särman speaks in her foreword – to believe in a system of truth, and when realising it is all made up of vague presumptions, to experience the curse of enlightenment.

If you don't want to think, this is not a book for you. If thought ever gave you pleasure, try to go beyond brightness.

From Annelie Bränström Öhman
Professor, Literary Studies and Gender Studies,
Department for Culture and Media Studies / Umeå Centre for Gender Studies, Umeå University, Sweden.

Sanja Särman's writing has a strange and beautiful allure. Portraying contemporary urban life in striking miniatures, she adopts the classic stance of tragic insight into the human predicament, and constantly oscillates between the loss of love and time and the gain of insight. In its most suggestive moments this choice of perspective reveals a sense of clarity that is both worrying and refreshing, like having a drink of cold spring water after waking from a nightmare; perhaps best described with the words of the protagonist in the eponymous short story, 'Beyond Brightness'. It is, "as if her eyes ... [are] microscopic lenses in some divine experiment".

From Laura Katherine Smith
PhD candidate in Literature and Culture at KU Leuven, Belgium.

With jarring sharpness, Särman's *Beyond Brightness* plunges the reader head-first into the lives of "ordinary people". Särman's prose – the juxtaposition of existential despair and lighting bolts of humour – cuts, her imagery shines, indeed with a strange, unnerving light. The short stories that make up *Beyond Brightness* deal with manipulation, jealousy, denial, existential insecurity, pride, hypocrisy, and the extent to which our lives can be "dangerously" intertwined or *bound to* – not only those physically around us, but our environments, the stories we tell ourselves, and the performances we play out – for ourselves and others. As such, the characters in these stories are "caught up" in whirlpools of intense relation. The air of palpable suffocation and the feeling of entrapment of the stories display the depth of desire and attachment that seem to have consumed their characters. Särman's writing succeeds in evoking a spatial *constriction*. The perception and point of view of these stories are fragmented and vertiginous; they are a harsh detail of existence, magnified. The intense emotions – be they jealousy, manipulation, or even detachment – are depicted with extremity. By casting fragmented yet electric details of human interaction into the stark light of centre-stage, the tense undercurrents of human emotion become Lautrec-like illustrations. *Beyond Brightness* strikingly reads as a lasting impression of *colour* – revealing the author's *other* passion: painting. The scarlet bloodstain on the lover's floor, the lonely father's pink plastic slippers, the silly wig of an older seductress, ripped off in lust – these ordinary-extraordinary details of shock burn themselves in the mind of the reader in a humorous and yet eerily *inevitable* manner.

From Yeeshan Yang
Author of *Whispers and Moans* and *Pelma's Tears*.

This fascinating book, *Beyond Brightness* – a collection of eleven short stories from Sanja Särman – portrays a world created from the perspective of her own observations of sensuality. Although most of her characters appear to be ordinary people living their mundane lives, the wide coverage of interactions between cultures in various corners of society gives increased depth and colour to each character, creating a multiplicity of meanings. This unpretentious method stimulates readers' imagination, as the author knows how to address her intellectual readers, and leave them wanting more. In fact this method of creative writing requires a deep understanding of human culture, acquired from life experience and observation.

I read each story in this collection as a deep interpretation of a particular situation or event, interested in each character's dilemma, and in the intelligent analysis of culture, as presented through the author's own observations. The actual world is separated into nationalities and cultures; the author uses the advantage of her own rich cultural background to seek to remove such separation by enhancing cultural understanding.

The writing in *Beyond Brightness* is successful, particularly for "intellectuals" who handle "unpretentious" stories with a "high culture" satisfaction. Designing a plot in storytelling should not simply be understood as a means to produce a "popular cultural product". On the contrary, plotting delivers emotions to engage readers so they can relate to the characters and situations portrayed by authors. Once a suitable emotion is delivered, readers will open their hearts to receive the messages unpretentiously conveyed by the author. Hopefully we will read more emotions in future works by Sanja Särman.

29 October 2016

NOTES

[i] "Slash": a phenomenon in which fans make unorthodox love couples out of fictional characters.
[ii] "SMV": Sexual Market Value

THE PUBLISHERS

Proverse Hong Kong (PVHK), founded by Gillian and Verner Bickley, is based in Hong Kong with long-term and developing regional and international connections.

Proverse has published novels, novellas, non-fiction (including autobiography and biography, diaries, history, memoirs, sport, travel narratives), single-author poetry collections, children's, young adult, and academic books. Other interests include academic works in the humanities, social sciences, cultural studies, linguistics and education. Some Proverse books have accompanying audio texts. Some are translated into Chinese.

We welcome authors who have a story to tell, wisdom, perceptions or information to convey, a person they want to memorialize, a neglect they want to remedy, a record they want to correct, a strong interest that they want to share, skills they want to teach, and who consciously seek to make a contribution to society in an informative, interesting and well-written way. Proverse works with texts by non-native-speaker writers of English as well as by native English-speaking writers.

The name, "Proverse", combines the words "prose" and "verse" and is pronounced accordingly.

YOUR RESPONSE

We are interested to read your response to Sanja Särman's short story collection, *Beyond Brightness*. If you would like to do so, please give us a few sentences which you are willing for us to publish, describing your response to this book, sending them to <info@proversepublishing.com>.

If your comments are chosen to be included in our E-Newsletter or website, and if you send us your mailing address, we will select another title published by Proverse and send you a complimentary copy.

Unless you state otherwise, we will assume that we may cut or edit your comments for publication.

We will use your initials to attribute your comments.

FICTION PUBLISHED BY PROVERSE

Those who enjoy Sanja Särman's short story collection, **Beyond Brightness**, may also enjoy the following short story collections, novels, and novellas.

SHORT STORY COLLECTIONS

Odds and Sods, by Lawrence Gray. 2013.

The Shingle Bar Sea Monster and other stories, by Laura Solomon. 2012.

The Snow Bridge and other Stories, by Philip Chatting. 2015.

NOVELS and NOVELLAS

A Misted Mirror, by Gillian Jones. 2011.

A Painted Moment, by Jennifer Ching. 2010.

An Imitation of Life. 2nd ed, by Laura Solomon. 2013.

Article 109, by Peter Gregoire. 2012.

Bao Bao's odyssey: from Mao's Shanghai to Capitalist Hong Kong, by Paul Ting. 2012.

Black Tortoise Winter, by Jan Pearson. 2016.

Bright Lights and White Nights, by Andrew Carter. 2015.

cemetery – miss you, by Jason S Polley. 2011.

Cop Show Heaven, by Lawrence Gray. 2015.

Curveball, by Gustav Preller. Scheduled November 2016.

Death Has a Thousand Doors, by Patricia W. Grey. 2011.

Hilary and David, by Laura Solomon. 2011.

Hong Kong Hollow, by Dragoş Ilca. Scheduled 2017.

Instant messages, by Laura Solomon. 2010.

Man's Last Song, by James Tam. 2013.

Mila the Magician by Zhang Jian (Catherine Chin). 2014.
(English/Chinese bilingual edition.)

Mishpacha – family, by Rebecca Tomasis. 2010.

Paranoia (the walk and talk with Angela),
by Caleb Kavon. 2012.

Red Bird Summer, by Jan Pearson. 2014.

Revenge From Beyond, by Dennis Wong. 2011.

The Day They Came, by Gérard Louis Breissan. 2012.

The Devil You Know, by Peter Gregoire. 2014.

**The Monkey in Me: Confusion, Love and Hope
Under a Chinese Sky**, by Caleb Kavon. 2009.

The Perilous Passage of Princess Petunia Peasant,
by Victor E. Apps. 2014. (Young adult fiction.)

The Reluctant Terrorist: in Search of the Jizo,
by Caleb Kavon. 2011.

The Village in the Mountains, by David Diskin. 2012.

Tiger Autumn, by Jan Pearson. 2015.

Tightrope! a Bohemian tale, by Olga Walló. 2010.
Translated from Czech by Johanna Pokorny, Veronika Revická & others.
Poetry translated by Justin Quinn and Veronika Revická.
Edited by Gillian Bickley & Olga Walló, with Verner Bickley.

University Days, by Laura Solomon. 2014.

Vera Magpie, by Laura Solomon. 2013.

FICTION – CHINESE LANGUAGE

The Monkey in Me, by Caleb Kavon.
Translated by Chapman Chen. 2010.

Tightrope! A Bohemian Tale, by Olga Walló.
Translated by Chapman Chen. 2011.
Chinese translation supported by the Ministry of Culture of the Czech Republic.

~~~

FIND OUT MORE ABOUT OUR AUTHORS, BOOKS, LITERARY PRIZES, AND EVENTS

Visit our website:
http://www.proversepublishing.com

Visit our distributor's website: <www.chineseupress.com>

Follow us on Twitter
Follow news and conversation: <twitter.com/Proversebooks>
OR
Copy and paste the following to your browser window and follow the instructions:
https://twitter.com/#!/ProverseBooks
"Like" us on www.facebook.com/ProversePress

Request our free E-Newsletter
Send your request to info@proversepublishing.com.

Availability
Most books are available in Hong Kong and world-wide from our Hong Kong based Distributor,
The Chinese University Press of Hong Kong,
The Chinese University of Hong Kong, Shatin, NT,
Hong Kong SAR, China.
Email: cup-bus@cuhk.edu.hk
Website: <www.chineseupress.com>.
All titles are available from Proverse Hong Kong
http://www.proversepublishing.com
and the Proverse Hong Kong UK-based Distributor.

We have **stock-holding retailers** in Hong Kong,
Singapore (Select Books),
Canada (Elizabeth Campbell Books),
Andorra (Llibreria La Puça, La Llibreria).
Orders can be made from bookshops in the UK and elsewhere.

Ebooks
Most of our titles are available also as Ebooks.

www.ingramcontent.com/pod-product-compliance
Lightning Source LLC
Chambersburg PA
CBHW051345020726
47501CB00007B/2282